What 1

MW01245039

Jan Springer and Lauren Agony write about the intriguing planet of Paradise where it is a women's world, where they call all the shots... I think she is going to be a wonderful asset to this publisher.

- *Tracey West for The Road to Romance*

Ellora's Cave Publishing, Inc.
PO Box 787
Hudson, OH 44236-0787

ISBN # 1-84360-566-X

Edited by Raelene Gorlinsky.
Cover art by Scott Carpenter.

Warning: The following material contains strong sexual content meant for mature readers. *A HERO'S WELCOME* has been rated NC 17 erotic, by a minimum of three independent reviewers. We strongly suggest storing this book in a place where young readers not meant to view it are unlikely to happen upon it. That said, enjoy…

A HERO'S WELCOME

Written by

LAUREN AGONY & JAN SPRINGER

Chapter One

Sometime in the not so far future on a faraway planet…

Squeals of excitement rippling through the air prompted Annie Wilkes, Male Slave Doctor, to lift her head and see what was going on. She wasn't the least bit surprised to find five women trying to subdue a naked male slave in the hub square.

What did surprise her was the size of his penis. Unusually large, it bounced gallantly as he swiveled his bound legs up in an effort to kick at the women holding down his arms and head.

Annie had always fantasized about finding a male that big. A male she could dominate and use as her own personal sex toy. She licked her lips as lust rippled through her body.

The male struggled valiantly and she silently cheered him on. To her disappointment two of the women quickly grabbed the slave's legs and held him down on the ground.

Sweat beaded his muscular body. An ugly raw bullet wound marred the left side of his neck.

Annie forced her gaze away from the newly captured slave back to Cath, who stood stooped over beside her. Her mouth was warped in concentration as she tried to twist together the loose ends of a barbed wire fence that had rusted apart. Cath would know what was going on.

She was the slave catcher and trainer of their hub and owned all the incoming slaves.

"Cath, who is that male? I've never seen him before." She spoke casually. No use in letting Cath know she was interested in this male. It would only make her increase her price.

Cath's eyes narrowed as she followed Annie's gaze.

"That one's trouble. He's violent. Every woman in my crew has tried to mount him, but he won't let anyone do him."

"Where's he from? I don't see any markings."

"Found him in the Outer Limits. No brands. Most likely escaped the breeding camps when he was little. He's slated for castration. It'll make him more docile."

Annie bit her bottom lip in frustration.

"It seems such a waste. Males that big are rare."

"Might want to take a look at him after they're through with the castration. He got wounded when he was captured."

"Castration will prevent him from performing sexually for at least a few days." Annie pondered aloud.

Cath's head snapped up. "Do I detect a little interest in this slave?"

Annie's face suddenly flamed.

"My God! You want to fuck him, don't you?" Cath gasped.

Annie avoided Cath's amused smirk and looked over at the woman picking up the glowing castration knife from the crackling campfire.

Darn it. They were going to destroy him in a minute. She had to do something to stop them.

"Yes, I want to fuck him. Do me a favor. Don't castrate him. Not yet."

"I don't do favors, Annie. I'll want something in return."

Annie watched wide-eyed with frustration as the knife-wielding woman hunkered down over the struggling male. Impatience soared through her.

"Name your price later. I'll do whatever you want."

"He won't be a willing participant."

Annie forced herself to focus her attention back to Cath and winked. "They make the best kind."

Cath dropped the pliers and headed toward the scene.

Annie's heart crashed against her chest as she watched the knife lower to the man's genital area.

"Hold off on that castration!" Cath yelled.

The gleaming knife stopped a mere inch from the man's scrotum.

Annie sighed in relief. Quickly she followed Cath, all the while cursing herself for what she'd just done.

What in the world had come over her? She'd never saved a slave from castration before. Never felt the need.

When she reached the group, Annie's gaze immediately latched onto his massive penis. Obviously the women had been amusing themselves with him. Despite the fact he was weak from his neck wound, his hard shaft stuck out fully erect waiting to plunge itself into her aching cunt. How powerful would he be inside her when he recovered? The thought enticed Annie to no end.

The women let the male loose. Muscles blazed to life in his upper thighs as he wasted no time getting into a defiant crouched position. More muscles rippled in his arms as he drew his bound legs up to cover the massive penis she'd been staring at.

As she studied this newcomer's naked physique, she sensed he was different.

Immediately she was drawn to his face. To his straight nose, the curve of his strong jaw line and the sexy shadow of stubble covering his cheeks and chin. His mouth appeared hard, determined, his lips full and lush.

She noticed he was staring back at her, his green eyes snapping with anger.

Annie shuddered. She'd expected to see fear in the male's eyes. Not anger.

This was quite interesting. He acted as if he knew what they'd been planning to do to him. As if intelligence brewed within him. But that wasn't possible. Males weren't supposed to be smart. They were stupid creatures bred for their strength and farmed for sexual purposes. They weren't even educated anymore. They were more manageable that way.

The way Green Eyes had fought so valiantly meant he retained some sort of brainpower. Perhaps he'd been secretly taught by a woman. She'd heard stories about those type of females. How they became attached to the male offspring forced upon them by the dreaded fucking machines. About how the female prisoners rescued their offspring from their fate as male slaves and disappeared into the surrounding forests to never be heard from again.

Excitement rippled through her. Was this male one of them? Did he understand what was going on around him? It wouldn't be to his advantage if he did understand.

Women didn't want smart males. They wanted docile sex slaves.

But with a massive rod like his, the women of the hub and many other hubs would be lining the streets for the pleasure he would bring them. He could be a king among slaves. Well looked after. And she would be able to visit him whenever she wished.

"Annie, where do you want to fuck him?" Cath's question broke into her thoughts.

Annie's face heated up again as the women standing around smirked and elbowed each other.

"I don't think he's in any condition for that right now, Cath. His wound needs tending."

"Shit, Annie. I thought you wanted a go at him."

Annie couldn't help but to notice the male watching her. Betrayal lurked in his green eyes. For the first time in her life she felt guilty. Guilty at wanting to mount a man who obviously didn't want to be mounted.

Why should she even care what he was thinking of her? Or care what he wanted? He was a male. Males were bred to serve women.

"If you don't want to fuck him then—" Cath took the knife from the other woman's hand and started toward the defiant slave.

Annie grabbed her elbow, stopping her cold.

"What the hell are you doing?" Cath spat. Yanking her arm free from Annie's desperate grasp, Cath held up the knife in a defensive gesture. Annie's blood froze in fear and Cath's slave training crew murmured excitedly at this unexpected turn of events. No one went up against Cath. No one told her what to do.

And no one ever touched her. Not unless she wanted them to.

Annie might just have ruined any chance of helping out this slave. She needed to do something. And fast.

"I hate to pull rank on you, Cath, but if you force me, I will." Annie couldn't believe how steady her own voice sounded.

Despite that, her insides quivered at her unexpected boldness.

"Shit, woman. What has gotten into you?" Cath spat.

"I don't see your brand on him, Cath."

"I told you why. And don't bother trying to claim him. He's mine. I shot him."

"As the Slave Doctor of this hub, it is my duty to remove an injured slave if I deem his life is in danger." Annie's heart began to thump wildly. She'd never stood up to Cath before. No one in their right mind would. It wasn't beneficial to have Cath as your enemy.

"What are you saying, Annie? You're taking my slave?"

"You said I could fuck him. I say he can't be fucked in his condition."

"You think I can't take care of what's mine?" The hurt in Cath's eyes was quite evident.

"I didn't insinuate that at all—"

"Damn you! You remove him and it'll go down on my record. I've never had a mark against me."

"I'll keep him off the record. Just between you and me."

Annie held her breath and waited for Cath's answer.

Cath studied the male, her eyes narrowed with hatred. But Annie could hear the wheels grinding in Cath's head. If the slave allowed Annie to have sex with him, it meant he could be broken. And if she broke him he could be trained and that would bring her lots of money when she stuck him into the brothel.

Before Cath could give an answer, the male slave suddenly slumped over, unconscious.

The women were thrilled. Their excited shrieks filled the air and they quickly crowded over his prone figure, groping his genitals.

Annie's heart climbed into her throat at the sight. She couldn't blame them. A big sized male was virtually non-existent these days.

Shooing away the women, she crouched beside him and placed a couple of fingers to his neck. Her stomach did a little nauseating flip at what she discovered.

"Pulse is slow. He's burning up with a fever. I'll have to move him immediately, Cath. He might have blood poisoning."

"Shit!" Cath shouted. "There goes my perfect record."

"I'll keep him off the records...if he lives."

* * * * *

Joe kept his eyes closed and clenched his jaw as a soft hand moved seductively over his bare chest. Her touch felt good. Real good.

He wanted to open his eyes. To look into the face of the woman who touched him so gently. But he was afraid he might be dreaming. And he didn't want this dream to end.

Her hand moved lower. Over his belly.

He shuddered involuntarily as her warm fingers cupped his balls, lifting them, testing their weight.

Her gentle fingers let go and moved to his flaccid penis. They wrapped around his shaft and squeezed tenderly.

Blood pooled into his groin area. His penis jerked to attention and grew hard as if he were readying himself to plunge into her hot cunt.

A small startled gasp made him open his eyes. He blinked in confusion as a room he'd never seen before rolled into focus. A sterile, white room. And it sure as hell wasn't a room in his spaceship.

What the hell was going on? Where was he?

In an instant the memories hit him like a body blow.

Shit!

After a year in hyperspace, he and his two brothers had finally landed on the planet they'd been sent to explore.

An unmanned space probe had discovered the planet a couple of years ago. Before losing contact with NASA, the probe had sent back sporadic and disturbing images.

Disturbing in the fact this newly discovered planet resembled the terrain and atmosphere of Earth, including an orbiting moon as well as various types of space junk. Space junk that indicated intelligent life existed or had existed at one point in time.

Because Joe and his two scientist astronaut brothers had been involved with helping to invent hyperspace travel, NASA had asked if they might be interested in the top-secret mission.

All three had readily agreed to participate, including agreeing to not make physical contact with any potential inhabitants and on the off chance they did, not to ask questions to arouse their curiosity. It was one of NASA's prime directives not to interfere with another race or let them know they were being studied until such a time as it was deemed the inhabitants were friendly enough to secure some type of diplomatic relations.

The three of them hadn't been on the planet for more than a week when his two brothers hadn't come back from a day of exploring. Efforts to contact them on the comm-link had failed.

When they still hadn't returned by the next morning, impatience had spurred him to go looking for them. He'd searched all day throughout the area where they were supposed to have been and hadn't found so much as a footprint.

Exhausted, hot, worried, and totally pissed off at not finding them, he'd heaved a sigh of relief when he'd spotted the gushing blue river up ahead. Within minutes he'd stripped, thrown his clothing and equipment into some nearby bushes, and plunged into the refreshing river.

The cool liquid had dulled his muscle aches and tempered his worry about his brothers as he'd leisurely floated down the river. When he'd climbed out of the water about two hundred yards downstream, he'd been felled by the bullet.

He still remembered the painful impact to his neck as the bullet had slammed into him, remembered falling onto the rocky shore. Most of all he remembered the women surrounding him, with their lusty smiles as they'd excitedly groped his shaft.

They knew exactly where to touch to arouse the hell out of him. Heck, it hadn't taken much since he'd been without female companionship for more than a year, but when they tried to mount him without his permission, he'd fought them off.

In thanks they had tied his arms and legs to a pole. Then they'd hoisted the pole with him on it and strung him between two females as if he were a recently killed deer or something. As they carried him, he'd drifted in and out of consciousness.

He had no idea how long he was tied to the pole, but however long it had been, his body was sore and raging with fever by the time they'd dropped him in the dirt and released him from the restraints.

And then the women had swarmed him again.

He'd fought as they'd touched him. They'd done a damn good job arousing him, but then he'd seen that sharp glowing knife heading for his balls.

His balls!

Joe bolted upward. Restraints tugged at his wrists and ankles, pulling him back against the mattress and a soft pillow.

Raw anger burned within him.

He wanted to shout, to demand he be untied. But his throat hurt like hell from the bullet wound. The only sound that escaped was a pathetic groan.

Then he noticed her.

She sat on the bed beside him and damned if she wasn't gently stroking his penis and his balls, her touch arousing him like crazy. Obviously he was still very much intact down there.

Relief spread like wildfire throughout his system, allowing him to contain his anger and survey the woman.

Wow, but she was a pretty one. Tangled curly brown hair framed her sweetheart-shaped face. A soft mouth pouted at him. A mouth he suddenly wanted to kiss.

Annie, that was her name. She'd been the one who'd quite literally saved his balls.

And for thanks she expected him to allow her to fondle him? Expected him to fuck her?

He felt the anger tighten his body.

"Easy, Green Eyes, easy."

Her sweet voice flowed over him like melted honey and he relaxed despite the lust he saw brewing in her eyes.

Glorious soft blue eyes fringed by long thick black eyelashes. She smelled fresh and clean and of strawberries. But how could he smell strawberries? He was a light year away from Earth.

Shit! He must be in some erotic dream. A damned good dream because this luscious dame was giving him the hardest hard-on of his life.

Not to mention she was totally naked.

Chapter Two

That's what this was. A dream. A reality dream. It had to be. She was too gorgeous to be real.

His brothers must have programmed her into his sleeping cubicle on their spaceship. He must have dreamt everything.

Getting shot.

The women.

Annie.

No, it couldn't be a dream. The arousal coursing through his shaft was too real. Too painfully pleasant.

"You'll be all right, Green Eyes. A little infection is all it was. I've given you a Quick Healing Injection. You need some rest and you'll be good as new."

Annie released his penis. He wished she hadn't. Her fingers felt good wrapped around his hard flesh. As if she belonged there.

His rod hardened even more as his gaze raked her curvy body. Her breasts were beautiful and full and so velvety looking. Not too big. Not too small.

Her aureoles were dusky colored. Her nipples large and suckable.

The thought of cupping her breasts in his palms made Joe's heartrate quicken. Damned if he could remember ever being more aware of a woman in his entire life.

"I don't know why I'm even talking to you. You don't understand a thing I'm saying," she murmured.

Leaning closer she lifted his bound wrist and took his pulse.

Her breasts were right there in front of his face. He found himself licking his lips in anticipation. He hadn't had his mouth on a woman's breasts in a long time. Hell, he hadn't been with a woman in a long time.

If he were to pick a woman to have some sex with, this one would be her.

Besides, he owed her. Big time. She'd stood up to the bitch who'd shot him. Taken charge of a bad situation and saved his balls.

She let go of his wrist and placed a cool hand against his forehead. Her soft touch was heaven.

"Your fever's gone. That's very good news." She smiled down at him with robust lips. Lips meant for kissing. Lips meant for sucking.

His penis stiffened at that idea.

She sure noticed his reaction, because her gaze slid down to his now fully erect cock.

He didn't miss the soft curve of her elegant throat move as she swallowed. And he didn't miss the look of longing in her eyes. He'd seen that look in many women back on Earth, right before he'd bedded them.

The pink tip of her tongue peeked out of her mouth as she surveyed his penis. A pretty blush slipped across her high cheekbones.

Oh yeah, he wouldn't mind fucking this one.

It was as if she read his mind because suddenly she was leaning closer. Her full breasts thrust outward at him as if encouraging him to take a taste.

Her look was hot and intense and unmistakable. She wanted to have sex with him.

The idea brought an abundance of questions zipping through him.

Why did she seem different from the other women? Why didn't he have the same urge to fight her off as he had with the others? And why in hell was his head telling him to cave in to these chaotic feelings of arousal rushing through his body and simply allow her to do with him whatever she pleased?

His body answered that question quite nicely as he reacted to her closeness.

The warmth evaporating from her skin dissolved his weakness, replacing it with a rip-roaring hum of energy. Energy that would be put to good use giving this woman what she wanted.

She held his gaze with those seductive blue eyes and she said nothing as her hands clutched his naked shoulders.

Her fingers burned into his muscles and she levered one long leg over his lower body.

Slowly she began to squat over his hips and onto his rod that stood at attention like a stiff flagpole. Hissing between his teeth, he watched in awe as his entire hard length slowly disappeared between the swollen hot lips of her clean-shaven pussy.

He slid into her easily. Her cunt was wet and oh so tight as her muscles immediately embraced him.

His heart suddenly felt as if it were on fire from the erotic look splashing over her face. He found himself lost in her startling beauty, disoriented by the sensuous smile tilting her full lips.

She began to rock her curvy hips fiercely on top of him. Her sensuous movements made her cunt muscles contract wildly around his flesh, sending chords of desire roaring through his shaft and straight into his belly.

Amazing, he'd never seen a woman have an orgasm so damn fast.

His heart beat wildly against his bare chest as her pert nipples stabbed into his face.

How could he refuse such a delicious offering? She shuddered as he took one of those luscious pink buds into his mouth, stroking the hot tip with his tongue and giving it a good suck at the same time.

Her screams of arousal intensified, coming from deep inside her chest. The sexy sound encouraged him to suck harder.

Her hands came up off his shoulders and her fingers plunged into his hair, cupping the back of his head, pulling his face into her soft breast. He suckled on her nipple as she continued to gyrate her hips.

Her exotic movements made his penis rage with pleasure and he hardened inside her like a steel rod. He thrust his hips upward and she met his strokes head on.

Her moans grew and she pulled her body away allowing him to let go of her breast and grab some air.

She smiled down at him as she rode him sensuously. Her look was hot and frenzied. Her short auburn hair bounced delightfully with each movement.

Perspiration dampened her forehead. Blistered across her pink cheeks as she continued to take the pleasure from him, moaning and gasping with each swivel of her hips.

When he felt her cunt muscles begin to shudder violently with another oncoming climax, he slowed down his thrusts in an effort to drag out the pleasure.

She frowned prettily. Then he ground upward into her cunt again. Shoving in deep and making her climax in yet another frenzied explosion.

Finally he could hold back no longer. His body tightened erotically and he shot his hot sperm deep into her.

When he finished, she collapsed on top of him. Her full breasts flattened against his chest and her hot face buried into the curve of his neck.

"I won't let them have you. I promise," she whispered against his skin.

He couldn't help but sigh in relief at her words. Couldn't help but wonder why he'd just fucked a woman he knew nothing about.

But it had felt right. And oh so good.

She didn't move off him, so he stayed snugly inside her hot cunt and listened to the lullaby pounding of her heart as it beat in unison to his.

Both of them must have dozed off because suddenly he awoke to find her gazing down at him, her eyes wide with terror.

And that's when he heard it.

Voices of women. Excited murmurs intermingled with angry ones. And they were heading directly for the room he was housed in.

Annie's hand immediately flew to his left wrist and the restraint there.

He held his breath as she began to unbuckle it. A knock came at the door.

Joe's heart jammed into his throat as she stared down at him. Emotions warred in her blue eyes. Fear. Confusion.

She looked to the door and back to him again. Her fingers fought wildly with the restraint. It didn't budge.

Another round of knocks came at the door.

Defeat ripped into her eyes.

He groaned as her warm softness left his penis as she climbed off him.

With lightning speed she dashed across the small room, making it to a large microscope set on a counter. An instant later the door burst inward.

Joe cringed as he recognized that bitch named Cath, the same one who'd nailed him in the neck with a bullet yesterday. She walked into the clinic as if she owned the place. Damned if she wasn't naked herself. Obviously the women around here were very sensual creatures and not shy about their bodies.

She took one look at Annie bending over her microscope and grinned knowingly.

"Apparently the slave has regained his health. I hope you've been enjoying yourself with him."

"He's still not in any condition to fuck, Cath."

Joe groaned inwardly. No use denying they'd just had sex.

Annie's auburn hair was all tousled and her lips and nipples were swollen from his kisses. Besides, her face blushed a pretty pink. A dead giveaway she'd just been in the sack.

Cath didn't look at him but headed straight toward Annie in a threatening swagger.

He felt the bonds around his wrists and legs tighten as he found himself wanting to break free to protect Annie.

Annie on the other hand seemed unafraid as the woman reached out and cupped Annie's shaven pussy.

Annie closed her eyes and arched her lower body into Cath's hand, evidently aroused by the woman's touch.

Joe frowned in confusion. What the hell was Annie doing? Why was she allowing the woman to fondle her?

"You are so wet, Annie. No use denying you've been fucking my slave."

Annie bit her bottom lip and said nothing as the two women stared at each other. Messages snapped between the two. Messages he couldn't decipher.

Terror washed into Annie's eyes. A red blush of embarrassment stained her already pink cheeks.

Cath's thin lips curled in satisfaction.

He tried to shout at Cath. Wanted to yell at her to get away from Annie. Nothing erupted from his throat. Nothing except an awful raw pain and a sickly whisper.

Finally Cath uncupped Annie and brushed past her, slapping a piece of paper onto a nearby table.

"What is it?" Annie asked.

"Read it later. All the details are there. In short, this paper states he's mine. I'm here to pick up my property."

Joe tensed.

"He's still not well enough to travel, Cath."

"If he's well enough to be fucked, he's well enough to leave."

Cath whirled away from Annie and headed toward him. Something evil gleamed in Cath's gray eyes and he didn't much care for that satisfied smirk marring her face either.

Shit!

"Cath, you can't take him. He's still not healthy enough."

"He'll be fine."

Dread sliced through Joe when he spotted the glistening needle full of blue fluid in Cath's hand.

Oh man. Don't do this, lady.

"Now hold on, Cath." Annie pulled on the woman's arm, practically dragging her away from him.

Cath's face twisted into an evil mask and Joe literally saw Annie tremble and shrink away from Cath in fear.

Okay, so his only ally was literally dissolving right before him. This was not a good thing.

He was screwed. Quite literally.

A wiggle of panic cut through his thoughts and Joe once again pushed his bare legs and arms against his restraints. Suddenly the restraint holding his left wrist loosened. Not enough to set him free, but just enough so he could wiggle the metal belt buckle beneath his wrist and use the sharp edge of it to do some fast scratching into the wood bedframe where his wrist was latched.

"My crew is right outside, Annie. You give me trouble, I'll holler."

"He's my patient. You can't come in here and take him!"

"I can see he's co-operating quite nicely. Maybe you should have drawn the drapes and closed the windows before you climbed on him and started moaning like a bitch in heat."

"I was trying to get him to trust me."

Joe finished what he was doing with the belt buckle and frowned. If Annie was telling the truth, then he'd just been had.

A noise from close by made him lift his head just in time to feel the sharp needle prick into his upper arm.

The effects were immediate. Dizziness swept over him like a tidal wave. A split second later the lights went out.

Chapter Three

Annie's guts twisted into a painful knot as she watched two of Cath's male slaves lift the unconscious Green Eyes from his bed and drag him out the door.

"Where are you taking him?"

"It's all in the requisition on the table," Cath said as she brushed past Annie.

"He could still have a relapse, Cath. I'll be putting him on your record if something happens to him."

Annie held her breath as Cath stopped short and whirled around. Anger and hurt flared in her eyes.

"I can't believe you pulled rank on me out there. I thought we were friends? I trusted you."

"We're still friends."

"I don't think so, Annie. You let a slave, a useless male, come between us. I never figured you'd do something so hideous."

Annie shrugged. Neither did she. She'd never been a fighter. Always a follower.

And then Green Eyes had shown up and everything had changed.

Watching him fight so valiantly against the women who'd wanted to castrate him had impressed her, had made something unexplainable flutter to life inside her heart. It had encouraged her to stand up to Cath. To stop him from being hurt.

Now that she'd fucked him, she knew she didn't want to lose him. He was the perfect sex toy.

The powerful upward thrusts of his hips had rammed his massive penis so deep inside her cunt, creating such violent waves of pleasure it had been literally breathtaking. A fantastic experience unlike anything she'd ever had before.

And she wanted more.

Hot tears burned at the back of her eyes prompting Annie to stroll over to the microscope on the counter. She peered into it, pretending to not care in the least that Cath had taken Green Eyes. She was determined Cath wouldn't see her cry.

Being so foolish as weeping over a male would only make her the laughing stock of the whole hub. And that's the last thing she wanted.

From behind her Cath inhaled a deep breath.

"He's not a pet," Cath continued. "He's a male. They're dangerous. They need to be restrained and watched at all times."

Footsteps crossed the floor away from Annie and then stopped. "It's a good thing I came along before you forgot those facts, Annie. I gotta go." The sound of the door slamming behind her made the hot tears in her eyes spill over.

With trembling hands she picked up the requisition Cath had left on the table.

Her mouth dropped open in shock. Of all the things she'd expected that Cath had taken him away for, it certainly wasn't this.

Annie blinked away the tears and prayed she was seeing wrong. The blurred words rolled into focus.

She bit her bottom lip in frustration as she read the words again.

Women's Prison Sperm Bank.

They'd taken Green Eyes to the Sperm Bank! He wouldn't survive in that horrid place. He was still too weak. Surely Cath wouldn't hurt him by bringing him there. She couldn't be so cruel.

Actually, she could. She was a bitch. Cath would hurt Green Eyes. Already had by shooting him. By having her women try to castrate him… Annie's stomach took a frantic plunge as she thought of something else. What if something went wrong in the Women's Prison Sperm Bank? What if one of those machines they hooked him up to went haywire? It was rare, but it happened.

She'd tended to some of those mutilated males. A malfunctioning machine ruined his ability to perform sexually. If that happened to Green Eyes he'd be reduced to working as a common laborer in the fields and he'd be put down the instant he couldn't work. Women had no patience for useless slaves. They were dealt with swiftly. Never coddled. But she'd coddled Green Eyes.

A fresh bubble of tears streamed down her face. In anger, Annie crunched the requisition in her trembling hand and threw it on the table.

She couldn't go against the hub. The order had come from the Queen herself. No one asked the Queen for a favor, not unless one was prepared to do some serious ass kissing.

Literally.

God! What was the matter with her? She shouldn't care one way or the other what happened to Green Eyes.

Caring for a male was forbidden. Fucking a male who didn't belong to you was a virtual death sentence. Although Cath had given verbal permission, she still could have lied and accused her of seducing her slave without her permission.

Annie had gotten off lucky with Cath. Very lucky.

Annie squared her shoulders and wiped away the hot tears. It had been pleasant having Green Eyes to play with, but fun time was over. She had work to do. Other patients to attend to.

She strode over to the bed Green Eyes had lain in and began to strip off the sheet. To her surprise the material still felt warm.

She pressed it to her face and inhaled. It smelled of Green Eyes. Of his wonderful masculine scent. A hint of the soap she'd used to bathe him. And the seductive scent of their lovemaking.

She clutched the linen tighter to her face.

Oh Green Eyes, I'm so sorry I failed you. So sorry.

A fresh wave of tears formed and reluctantly she drew the sheet away from her face. From the corner of her eye she noticed something scratched into the wooden side of the bed.

That hadn't been there before. She was sure of it. She'd spent so much time over the past few hours sitting right beside Green Eyes, nursing him and then fucking him. Certainly she would have noticed the message.

Annie leaned closer and blinked in confusion at the word etched into the wood.

SOS.

Shock zipped through Annie making her legs watery. She sank onto the bed.

SOS — the universal signal for help.

Could this be possible? Was this a message from Green Eyes? Could he actually communicate?

A wave of dizziness swept over her and she leaned over to breathe deeply of the fresh air flowing in through the open window.

The same window that had exposed her as she'd moaned while making love to Green Eyes. Annie looked down and saw the spatter of tiny wood shavings on the edge of the floor. Then she examined the buckle on the restraint that had held down Green Eyes' left wrist. The same restraint she'd tried to loosen only minutes earlier.

A small flake of wood was stuck on the edge of the belt buckle.

It had been Green Eyes!

The shock of this new discovery sent Annie crashing butt first onto the mattress. A horrible uneasiness slithered through her gut as she realized something.

The bullet wound in his neck!

It must have prevented him from speaking. But when it healed, he'd start talking. And the women of the hub would kill him.

Any males showing signs of intelligence were swiftly put to death. It was the law incorporated by all hubs on the planet. A law that had existed since the creation of the Inner Limits.

And since the male belonged to Cath, she would be responsible for killing Green Eyes. And she'd do it personally because Cath always used any excuse to kill a male. Cath's favorite saying was "The only good male is a dead male."

Chapter Four

Joe's teeth slammed together as another wild current ripped through his penis. Damn! This was the biggest jolt of them all. And it was making him quake with desire.

He'd awoken to find himself handcuffed by the wrists and ankles to a cozy bed. IV's were sticking into his arms and a large suction cup was strapped over his balls and rod. Inside the cup, something that felt eerily similar to fingers was kneading his balls and stroking his penis.

To his shock, his body responded madly to the violent ministrations of the machine. He'd been shooting loads left, right, and center since he'd arrived.

The kneading on his balls intensified and he jerked again. His penis hardened. Swelled. Ached.

The kneading stopped and he exhaled a sharp breath as he tried to relax.

He had no idea how long he'd been lying here. Could be two, maybe three days. However long it was, he hoped to hell Annie had found the message he'd scratched onto the bed frame. Hoped she could conjure up some way of getting him out of this madhouse.

He winced as angry screams ripped through the tiny cubicle he'd been housed in. The guards were bringing in another naked woman.

This woman was prettier than the last few. Prettier, younger, and in great shape. Just looking at her curvy buttocks, wide hips, narrow waist and shaved pussy got his heart racing and his shaft tightening painfully.

The thought had already occurred to him they'd probably shoved sex drugs into his IV. Every time he saw a new woman enter the room, he felt his rod stiffen tighter than it had ever done on its own.

The way this chick was fighting the techs gave him the impression she sure as hell didn't want to be here. Well, join the club, honey.

Despite her struggling they tossed her onto the other bed with ease.

"Easy does it, Virgin, I thought you were an old pro at this." The guard chuckled as the technician quickly clamped the cuffs over her wrists and shoved her butt up onto a padded ramp. Thrusting her legs into the air, they spread-eagled her and placed her feet into stirrups, cuffing her ankles securely into place.

A moment later one of the technicians screwed a giant dildo onto a metal rod that extended from the refrigerator sized machine. Then she smeared it with some yellow ointment and slid the giant dildo carefully into the blonde's cunt.

When the woman moaned, the technician stopped and grinned down at her.

"Looks like you're going to get another wonderful baby male put into your oven. Hopefully the wee one will get as big a rod as his daddy's. Don't worry though, your baby will get put to good use when he's old enough to start servicing, just like your other one."

"I don't want another male child!" she gasped.

The female technician chuckled. "Enjoy the fucking machine while you can, Virgin. After this bun's in the oven it'll be a long haul before the next session and the one after that—unless you agree to service me or the rest of the guards?"

"Go fuck yourself!" The woman spat at the technician.

"Easy now, Virgin. Or that machine just might develop a mind of its own. You wouldn't want that to happen, would you?"

Joe didn't miss the fear shudder through Virgin's slender body.

Near as he could figure, the women brought into this cubicle were some sort of prisoners. Instead of being sentenced to years they appeared to be sentenced to how many babies they produced.

The thought of his offspring being used as sex objects by these women made his stomach clench in nausea. At this point however, there really wasn't much he could do.

Protocol on Earth dictated not to interfere with the inhabitants of this planet. Even though it was space law, it didn't mean he had to like it.

The blonde named Virgin turned her head toward him and saw him staring at her. Her sharp blue eyes shot sparks of hatred at him and her face scrunched up into an angry mask. "What are you looking at, slave?"

Okay, so the blonde had a great body. But she was just a wee bit too hostile for his taste. Maybe the fucking machine would put her into a better mood.

Joe gritted his teeth as the suction cup began kneading his balls again. Did this thing ever stop?

The machine had kept him aroused virtually 24/7. Never allowed him to fully fall asleep. It must have made him come at least six times today. And he was getting a wee bit sore down there.

He couldn't help but feel sorry for those cows back on Earth, their udders hooked up to milking machines day in and day out.

Speaking of udders and milking machines, the blonde was being outfitted with giant cone-shaped suction cups that fit over both her perky breasts. Once the cups were fitted snugly, the technician picked up a smaller suction cup and strapped it over the woman's pleasure bud.

The technician nodded to the guard, who walked over to the console and pressed a button.

Virgin gasped as her machine whirred to life. Joe watched in stunned fascination as the cones on the woman's breasts started to vibrate and the tiny suction cup positioned over her pleasure bud began to tremble. The fucking machine sprang into action. The dildo slid sensuously out and then into her cunt again.

A split second later a euphoric look flooded over Virgin's face and she scrunched her eyes closed. Joe did the same when his machine whirred to life.

He found himself gasping as the fingers began kneading harder on his balls. The now familiar stroking began up and down his shaft.

He forced his mind to concentrate on Annie. To pretend she was the one touching him, instead of those fake fingers in the suction cup groping his shaft.

He made himself believe it was Annie's wicked mouth wrapping around him, stroking him with her long tongue, sucking him. He gasped and writhed as she sucked harder.

The woman on the other bed moaned desperately as the dildo rammed in and out of her vagina.

Joe listened to her moans and pretended they were Annie's soft gasps as he slammed his hard rod into her warm pussy. God, he wanted Annie so bad he thought he would explode.

He clenched his teeth as his entire body tensed. For an endless moment he hung on the edge of a beautiful precipice, his body ablaze with pleasures he couldn't begin to describe. From out of nowhere the searing red-hot orgasm shot through his shaft with such a mind blowing force Joe moaned and released his load. The machine hummed louder as his sperm shot through the tube toward the dildo and Virgin.

Beside him Virgin gasped as his hot sperm shot straight into her cunt.

The suction cup eased off and Joe tried to relax. His job was done and he melted against the bed, perspiration drenching his entire body. Another climax like this, he'd drop dead of exhaustion.

Beside him the woman's moans slowly diminished and she grew quiet. They'd be coming to take her away soon. And it would start all over with another woman.

"Green Eyes?" Annie's soft voice came out of nowhere. For a moment Joe figured his mind had snapped. Broke from reality. Perhaps he was only imagining her voice. Maybe he had never left the clinic? Maybe this horrid place was a fever induced dream?

"Green Eyes." The voice came again. This time it was lower. An urgent whisper.

Joe groaned inwardly. If Annie had come to rescue him, she sure was getting an eyeful.

A warm hand touched his bare arm and he jolted. It felt strange to be touched by a warm woman. So strange, it hurt.

His eyes snapped open. His heart picked up speed when he spied Annie standing beside his bed looking down at him. Her sweet smile made a sharp pang of emotions grip his heart.

She was here! Dammit! She was here!

"I came to warn you, Green Eyes."

Warn him?

"Don't communicate with anyone. Do you understand me?"

He blinked in confusion, opened his mouth to try to say something.

Her reaction was immediate and swift. Eyes wide with shock she pressed a warm finger to his lips and hissed into his ear.

"Don't speak. It's illegal. Keep quiet!"

Illegal? What the hell?

"A little bit of foreplay, Annie?"

Joe tensed as Cath's amused voice made Annie's finger stiffen on his lips. She threw him a warning look that might have made his shaft wither if he hadn't already just come.

Annie straightened to attention and planted an awesome smile on her full mouth.

"Cath! I've been looking for you."

"You seem to have found your little patient too. Can't seem to keep your hands off him either, can you?"

"You're right. I can't."

Joe's stomach dropped in disappointment. That's all Annie had come for? Another fuck? Come to think of it, she hadn't said she was here to get him out.

"I have a requisition form." Annie said and held out a piece of paper.

Cath frowned and snatched it from Annie's fingers.

Joe managed to relax a little. Okay, so maybe he'd been wrong about Annie. Maybe she had a plan.

"How'd you secure this deal? A little ass kissing with the Queen?"

Annie stiffened at Cath's remark.

"Well, Annie. I had to do it too. Just to get him back from you. Looks like we've got a little war on our hands."

"Looks like."

Joe studied Annie's stern face. She didn't appear to cower under Cath's intense stare as she'd done the other day.

Atta girl, Annie. Looked like she'd picked up some courage over the past couple of days.

"This requisition states you don't get him until tomorrow morning."

Tomorrow morning? Shit, he could be dead by then with all these mind-blowing orgasms.

"I decided to come in a little early. Make sure you're taking great care of him."

"A man his size is gonna cost a big favor for the Queen and me, Annie. You think you can handle the fee?"

"The Queen has my answer. I can discuss the details with you when you have the time." Annie peered down at the suction cup clamped over Joe's penis.

Oh man! Was this embarrassing or what?

"What setting have you got him on, Cath?" Annie's voice was concerned.

He held his breath as Annie unstrapped the cup and stroked his penis. Damned if her soft touch wasn't getting him all wound up again.

"A six. You said go easy on him."

"Haven't your people been lubricating him? He's as red as a lobster. He looks a little sore."

Cath came over and examined his penis. Thank God, she didn't touch him. He might have lost his head, found his damn voice and shouted at the bitch to keep her dirty hands off him.

"I'm sure he'll be more than a little sore when you get through with him."

Joe didn't miss the nudge Cath gave Annie and he sure as hell didn't miss Annie's little smile.

His stomach dropped again. Was Annie getting him out of here just so she could climb on top of him and start screwing him again?

"I was hoping you might release him a little earlier."

"I can't do that. I've got the entire Cell Block C getting impregnated by his sperm tonight. Word's gotten around that he's big. Most prisoners are even volunteering to have his offspring. I've made more money off this slave in the last three days than the entire last three years."

"I'm happy for you, Cath. Truly I am."

Cath seemed to smile at Annie's soft spoken words.

"How about I buy you a refreshment, Annie? We can talk about the conditions the Queen set."

Annie nodded. She threw Joe a quick glance.

He shuddered at the look of despair in Annie's blue eyes. Exactly what were these conditions Cath was talking about? Whatever they were, Annie didn't look as if she liked them.

She turned away from him and followed Cath out the door, leaving Joe feeling totally abandoned.

He sucked in a sharp breath as those seductive fingers inside the suction cup began to knead his balls again.

Chapter Five

Annie popped the freshly baked bread out of the hot oven and quietly closed the door. Peeking over her shoulder, she breathed a sigh of relief to find the naked Green Eyes still sleeping soundly on the bed where Cath's women had dumped him an hour ago.

She'd been surprised that Cath and the workers had come so early with the unconscious Green Eyes. The sun wasn't even up yet. Unfortunately the sly grin on Cath's face made it obvious she was eager to please Annie, especially since Annie had agreed to all the conditions the Queen had asked for.

Annie frowned. She didn't know why she was so nervous. He was a male. A slave. He was here to fuck her. To do to her whatever she wanted done. And yet he could communicate. Proved it by leaving the SOS on the bed frame. That fact frightened her and excited her at the same time.

Her gaze came to rest on his massive penis lying asleep on top of him. It was still red. Very tender. Obviously Cath hadn't applied the salve Annie had suggested. The woman was mean to her slaves. She hadn't always been that way. She'd been a nice enough person until last year's Slave Uprising.

The Uprising had changed Cath. It had made her angry, distrustful of the males. Made her violent with the slaves and with everyone around her. Everyone hated Cath. Everyone but the Queen.

Despite Annie's hatred for Cath, Annie had kept up the friendship over the past year. Cath had connections that Annie needed. She was the Queen's main mate for one. And she was the governor of the Women's Prison.

Those connections had almost been lost because of her stand against Cath over the slave. But last night she'd proven to Cath how loyal she was.

Annie clasped her arms over her breasts as a shudder of revulsion ripped through her. She'd done what Cath and the Queen had asked of her, because of Green Eyes. And because of Cath's connections.

Connections Annie hoped would soon get her out of her Slave Doctor assignment and transferred to work at the Women's Prison. She wanted to be at the prison's clinic. She wanted to bring those prisoners' babies into the world. Wanted to hold the wee ones in her arms and cuddle them. Especially since she'd never be allowed to have one of her own, unless she did something against the law and was actually sentenced to a baby.

But even then she wouldn't be able to keep the baby she produced. Laws strictly prohibited the mother and child to bond for longer than two months. That's when mother and child were separated. If the mother's sentence was completed, she was released from prison. Otherwise she stayed to continue her sentence and was impregnated immediately with her next child.

A girl baby was placed with nurturers and eventually educators, who would choose an appropriate career the female would pursue. A male was placed with nurturers and then with slave trainers who taught the males to obey simple orders.

Annie found herself wondering how a child conceived with Green Eyes might look like. Would a girl have the same brilliant green eyes? Would a male be as powerfully built?

Memories of them together on his clinic bed flashed through her mind. Memories of her straddling his muscular hips. Gasping shamelessly as his massive rod speared deep into her cunt, filling her as she'd lowered herself onto him. Of his hot, wet mouth clamping tightly over her aching nipple.

His groans had sounded so erotic as she'd undulated her hips against him. He'd brought such pleasure to her. She wanted to experience the fantastic desire again. Wanted to feel his hot sperm shoot into her womb.

She'd kept their sheets. Put them on her bed. The aroma of their lovemaking had sifted out of the material and filled her nostrils during the nights he'd been in the Sperm Bank.

Now she had him back. It had come at a high price. But he was here.

And she was afraid to wake him. To take him, like she'd so brazenly taken him in the clinic.

Annie bit her bottom lip and tiptoed to the chair beside his bed with every intention of simply watching him sleep.

Unfortunately his colossal penis beckoned. Since he'd arrived this morning, she hadn't been able to keep her hands off it. Perhaps it was because of his size. Or maybe because she knew how sore he would feel when he awoke.

Annie dipped her fingers into the yellow salve lying on the night table and gingerly wrapped her fingers around his smooth, limp shaft. Using her other hand she sensuously rubbed the creamy salve up and down his inflamed rod. To her surprise, his cock thickened powerfully in her hands and lanced straight up from his belly.

"Not that I'm complaining, but we've got to stop meeting like this."

The amused sound of a masculine voice shocked her brain and she jerked around to find Green Eyes watching her.

A split second later fear cleaved into her spine as she realized she hadn't tied his hands or his feet to the bed.

He must have noticed, because he suddenly sat bolt upright.

He was free.

Free slaves were dangerous.

Annie struggled to inhale air into her lungs. Her gaze searched frantically for a weapon and she spied the bread knife lying on the table across the room.

She was halfway out of the chair when his strong fingers clasped over her wrist like a handcuff. Memories of last year's Slave Uprising rained down on her and a bad case of the shakes slammed into her full force.

"Let go of me!"

"Annie! It's okay!"

He tried to wrap his arms around her waist. Panic welled up and broke free from her. She pushed against his chest with all her might until he fell backward. He groaned as his back smashed hard against the wall.

Annie leapt from the chair and ran for the knife.

She didn't make it far. He caught her arm and tugged hard. She couldn't believe his strength as she found herself whirling around and slamming into his hot naked length.

Panting, she twisted in his arms and tried to break free. But his arms were too powerful, his chest a wall of cement.

She couldn't break loose!

"Please, let me go. Don't hurt me!" She pleaded.

"Calm down, Annie! I'm not going to hurt you." His voice sounded low and soothing but did nothing to squash the fear rampaging through her insides. She continued to struggle.

Suddenly he gripped her chin. In an instant his mouth brushed against her lips in a soft caress that sent a whisper of desire ripping through her terror.

Startled by his tenderness, Annie couldn't help but hope she was wrong about Green Eyes. A vague memory of his mouth sucking her breast pushed its way into her mind. He could have hurt her then. He hadn't.

The tenderness in his lips slowly turned to a desperate fierceness. Sensations ripped through her mouth and cunt like a bomb. It devastated her. Made her feel as if she were sinking into a whirlpool of sexual cravings.

Dark and dangerous cravings.

Ignoring the warnings in her head, she allowed her mouth to melt against his lips. He tasted mysterious and delicious. Of dominance and power. Of male.

Hot desire pounded through her veins, setting her body on fire. She found herself pressing her breasts against his muscular chest, gasping at the intimate gesture.

She arched against his strapping penis. She wanted him desperately. So much that it hurt.

Suddenly he broke the kiss and pressed his lips against the column of her neck.

"Now that I have your attention, how about you cutting me a slice of bread? I'm starving," he whispered.

Confusion cut a path through her desire. He wanted her to serve him bread? Serving a male was against the law. It was a sign of dominance. His over hers. A very bad thing.

To her surprise he let go of her, stepped away and handed her the knife.

A gesture of trust?

Trust she wished she could give him, but no matter how hard she tried, she couldn't. She'd never been around a male who hadn't been restrained in some way. Or a male who could speak more than one or two sentences at a time.

Green Eyes was dangerous. In more ways than one.

He wavered slightly and slumped into a chair, all energy seemingly draining from his body. Concern washed over her at his suddenly pale appearance. "Are…are you all right?"

"I'm afraid I'm not up to full par. If I was…" He let his words trail off, leaving a hot promise in its wake.

Annie found herself nodding numbly as the full impact of his words set in. He wanted to fuck her. She could see the lust in his eyes. Had felt it in the way he'd held her so closely. In the way he'd kissed her.

He craved food so he could gain strength. To gain power over her. To do with her what he wanted, instead of the other way around. And she would be powerless to stop him, just like the women of the hub had been powerless during the Slave Uprising.

She should attack him with the knife, wound him enough so she could subdue him. But he was expecting that. He would be on his guard.

On horribly trembling legs, Annie kept a wide berth from him and walked to the steaming bread she'd set on the counter only minutes ago.

Heart pounding against her chest, Annie lifted the knife and began to cut the bread.

"Do you have any jam? Butter?" His strong voice curled over her shoulder and she tensed. He'd come up behind her and she hadn't even heard him.

"We don't use butter. Not good for the heart. Berry Jam is in the cooler." She nodded toward the trap door in the floor. "Open the door. It's just inside."

She couldn't help but peek at him as his powerful naked form bent over. His back was toward her. His firm buttocks jutted out in a way that made her wish she could reach out and caress them.

He grasped the handle of the door in the floor and tugged.

Annie grabbed the nearest pot and crashed it over his head.

Chapter Six

Joe woke up to find the first rays of gray light seeping through the windows of the tiny one-room cabin. From a nearby open window, warm air spilled inside and curled over his body.

He wasn't surprised that it was warm. They'd been here one week and the planet's temperature had remained a steady 70 Fahrenheit during the night and wavered between 80 and 90 Fahrenheit during the day. Sunny days were the norm and from the look of the lush vegetation on the planet, it did rain just enough to keep the trees green.

The soft sound of someone breathing caught his attention and he spotted a woman's curvy body sitting in the chair beside his bed.

Annie.

Lovely black lashes framed her pretty eyes as she slept. To his disappointment she was still fully clothed. But her thin top left little to his imagination as he watched her full breasts rise and fall with her every breath.

The mere thought of what he wanted to do to her made the blood in his veins run hot and his shaft harden with need. His fingers itched to touch her velvety flesh. He craved to fill his palms with her plump softness. Ached to kiss the seductive swells of her breasts and suck valiantly on those precious nipples until her sweet gasps of delight filled the room.

Have mercy! Was he turning into some kind of a sex maniac? Or was there something else going on? Had they pumped him full of sex drugs before bringing him here? Is that why he was feeling so horny?

He sighed in frustration. Whatever the reason for his intense reactions to her, he needed to get out of here. Before he ended up making love to this luscious creature named Annie.

Unfortunately he couldn't do anything because once again he was lying on a bed with his wrists and ankles handcuffed to the bed's railings. And he was totally nude.

At least this time he wasn't in the clinic or the sterile cubicle in the Sperm Bank where anyone could walk in and do with him what they wanted. This place smelled clean and fresh like Annie, not of medicine and stale sickness.

He studied the brightening room and the sparse furnishings. Two sturdy twig chairs were pushed beneath a solid pine planked table. A coarse brown rug lay beneath it. A simple kitchen was nestled toward the far wall. Cabinets were made of knotty pine. A gray slate stone was being used as a countertop. And the floor was planked wood. The walls, square logs, were chinked with dry moss.

Everything appeared to be handmade. Including the charcoal drawings that hung on the walls.

Maybe this was Annie's home, although he didn't think so. He pictured her as having wildflowers in a vase and colorful drapes and cozy furniture. And no clothing on her gorgeous body. Yet it was the other way around. She wore the clothes and he wore nothing.

He felt miserable being chained to a bed. Not being able to roam freely or to touch her was getting on his nerves.

Yet Annie slept as peacefully as if he wasn't even in the room.

Interesting.

Earlier when he'd awoken to find her silky fingers wrapped around his aching shaft, his simple comment about how they kept meeting like this had sent a wave of terror washing over her pretty face. She had run from him and when he'd grabbed her, she'd begged him not to hurt her. He'd been stunned by her reaction and had tried to quench the panic by giving her a reassuring kiss. He'd hoped to remind her of their fantastic coupling in the clinic. He'd given her the knife as a show of trust.

It hadn't worked. The instant his back was turned, she'd whacked him right over the head, knocking him out cold.

Now he was back to square one. Cuffed helplessly to the bed and with a sore-as-hell shaft aching for her tender touch. Not to mention a headache the size of Mt. Everest.

And dammit, he wanted out of this bed!

In sudden anger he yanked at the handcuffs. Pain sliced through his wrists and the entire bed creaked ominously.

"What are you doing?" Annie blinked wildly from her perch on the chair.

"I'm getting pissed off, Annie." He growled, truly getting ticked at hearing the fear in her voice. "I don't know why you hit me. Or why you're so scared of me. Quite frankly at this point I don't give a rat's ass. I just want to leave, okay. Just cut me loose so I can leave."

"I can't do that."

"Why the hell not? Isn't that why you got me out of that madhouse? Or...would you prefer that I fuck you first?"

The soft inhale of her breath gave her away. "You make it sound so harsh."

"So that's what you want. You snap your fingers and expect a man to begin fucking you. You say stop, he stops. Where's the fun in that? How about switching roles?" At that suggestion, her eyes widened with shock.

"That's illegal!"

"Just like a man speaking his mind is illegal. What the hell kind of world is this anyway?"

Realizing he'd given too much away, he clammed up. He needed to rein in his anger or he'd be spilling all the beans. The last thing he wanted was for her to find out he was from another planet.

A pretty little wrinkle burrowed between her eyebrows as she watched him with curiosity.

"Educating males hasn't been done in decades. Which outlaw female taught you?"

Outlaw female? Ookay. Whatever.

"Just let me go and pretend you never saw me."

"I can't. You belong to the Queen now. You are a slave."

"Fine. I'm a slave. Just untie me and I'll do what you want," he lied. The minute she untied him he was out of here.

She shifted uncomfortably in her chair and avoided his gaze.

That pretty pink blush stained her cheeks again and a large part of him wished she'd climb on top of him and sink her heat over his sore penis, like she'd done in the clinic. Another part of him wanted her to trust him. Wanted her to undo the cuffs, so he could make proper love to her, like a man should do to a woman he cared for.

Joe cursed inwardly at that thought. Caring? How the hell could he care for a woman who was afraid of him? A woman who cowered away from him when he was free to be a man.

"You think I'm dangerous when I'm free, don't you? That's why you hit me."

"I...I'm sorry. I shouldn't have hit you so hard."

"You shouldn't have hit me at all, Annie. I'd never hurt you."

Through the early morning light, he saw her frown deepen. Noticed her fists knot in her lap.

"Untie me, Annie. I'll prove to you I won't harm you."

"I can't."

"You don't trust me."

She hesitated. That was a good sign.

"The other day. At the clinic. When we...made love. I could have hurt you then. But you trusted me with your breasts. You let me bring pleasure to you with my mouth. I showed you then that you weren't wrong to trust me. Let me go and I'll show you again."

"It's against the law to allow a male loose without restraints."

So that was the problem. The women ruled the roost around here. That answered his question why he hadn't seen any men walking around.

"But you almost undid my restraints in the clinic the other day. You almost let me go. Why?"

"I...I lost control. It won't happen again."

Shit!

"Okay, okay. Have it your way. But how about some food? I'm starving. I haven't eaten a decent meal since I got caught. And um...I need to use the bathroom...or the outhouse...or the nearest tree."

"You'll have to use this basin for your...personal care," she said as she dug under the bed and brought out an odd looking ceramic basin with a hollow pipe sticking out of it.

Joe clamped down on his suggestion of what she could do with that basin.

When her warm fingers intimately wrapped around his hard shaft he gritted his teeth together to prevent himself from moaning at the desire her touch created.

His face flamed with embarrassment as she guided his flesh into the large pipe. He found little satisfaction at the pink flush blaze across her cheeks while he urinated into the basin. When he was finished she even tapped his rod for him.

Have mercy! When he got out of these cuffs, he sure as hell was going to exact some sort of sweet revenge on her for putting him through this humiliation.

He watched her open the door and step out into the early morning gray. A moment later she came back in without the basin.

In the kitchen she washed her hands using a pitcher and bowl and then went to work. Pots clattered and she hummed in a low tune as she worked on a meal for him.

Soon the delicious aroma of bacon and eggs drifted beneath his nostrils.

Over the last few days, he'd observed the similarities to Earth on this planet. Wondered how these people had been taught English. Wondered who'd supplied them with the guns that looked oddly similar to the ancient weapons produced on Earth.

He'd noticed right off something wasn't quite as it should be when he'd been shot and then awoken to find the women giggling and fondling his penis.

He wondered how his brothers, Ben and Buck, had fared. Had they been captured too? Is that why they hadn't returned to the spaceship? Heaven help him if anyone hurt his younger brothers in any way. He'd kill them first and ask questions later.

"Here you go." She placed a tray into his lap and sat beside him on the bed.

He gazed down at the crisp bacon, steaming eggs and apple slices arranged neatly on the tray and suddenly felt ravenous. "You going to let my hands loose so I can eat?"

Her pretty blue eyes narrowed warily.

"How about one hand?" he prodded.

A sweet little smile brightened her face and the metamorphosis surprised Joe. To his surprise his heart did a strange little twist. It was a feeling he rather liked.

"Okay. One hand," she agreed.

Cautiously she placed a key into the cuff, turned it, and the cuff snapped open. Quickly, she stepped back out of his reach.

"Well, this is a start," he said, trying hard not to get his hopes up.

Picking up the fork he stabbed a piece of crisp bacon and raised it to his mouth. It was hot and the best damned bacon he'd ever tasted in his life. Even better than his mom's, and mom's was the best. He didn't waste any time with compliments on her cooking. He was hungry and he figured she'd get the idea that she was a great cook by the way he wolfed it down.

When he was finished, he looked up to see her watching him intently with a luscious smile on her full lips.

"It was great," he said.

"I'm glad you liked it."

He lifted the tray and held it out to her. Holding his breath, he waited for her reaction.

She stared at him. Long and hard. As if trying to figure out what her next move should be. And then finally she moved. With great wariness, she reached out and took the tray, her fingers brushing erotically against his hand. Hot sparks snapped against his skin where she touched and he flinched at the intensity. She must have been experiencing the same reaction because he heard her sharp inhalation.

To his surprise she broke the contact, placed the tray on the chair and moved closer to him. So close that his outstretched hand came into contact with her belly.

He felt her tremble at his touch. Instinctively he knew it wasn't out of fear, but out of want. For him. Did she want him so bad she was willing to throw caution to the wind? Or was this her way of testing him? Of finding out if she could trust him?

It took every ounce in his being to not grab her, pull her against him and force her to uncuff his other hand.

Instead, he followed his instincts and spread his hand over her velvety belly. Allowing it to rest there for a moment, he relished the warmth her flesh created.

Beneath his touch she softened against his hand and that's when he slid his fingers beneath her flimsy shorts.

Chapter Seven

The instant Green Eyes' hand touched her abdomen, Annie's body was lost in a firestorm of lust. Gone were the feelings of fear and anger, insanely replaced by a pleasure so powerful it dazed her brain into moving closer to him. His was a body she wanted to fuck again. No matter what the consequences.

Wet liquid pooled between her legs as his warm fingers slid beneath her pants. He glided over her abdomen and then his hand stilled.

Puzzled, she looked down at Green Eyes. At the dark shadow of stubble shadowing his face. It made him look sexier, more dangerous, rough.

His full lips pouted up at her. The sulky gesture aroused her and she wanted to taste those warm lips.

His green eyes flashed with need and with anger.

Anger at not having his freedom. She wasn't used to that look. The look of a man who craved freedom. It just wasn't normal.

She became lost in his green eyes and adrift in the pleasure his hot fingers created as he began to move again. Tension zipped through her cunt. Instinctively Annie widened her legs.

She moaned as his fingers raked across her pleasure bud. Winced as he hit the sensitive area on her clit.

He stopped. "What's happened here?" he asked as his finger caressed the metal object.

In the heat of the moment she'd forgotten about it.

"A ring?" he asked.

Annie fought back the anxiety. She feared he wouldn't like what they'd done to her.

"It's a clit ring."

"It wasn't there before."

"I had it done. Last night. For you," she lied.

Actually she hadn't had much choice in the matter. It was tradition when taking a female mate. For her it was just another stepping stone to achieve her dream job. But he didn't have to know about that part.

Her heart hammered against her chest as she waited for his response.

"Does it hurt?" he whispered.

Did she detect a pleased note in his voice? Or was she only wishing he liked what she'd allowed them to do.

"No," she lied.

Actually the quick healing injection would take effect within an hour or two and she would be completely healed by this evening.

He began to rub softly around the painful area. Annie closed her eyes and drifted with the sharp conflicting sensations of pleasure and pain. Without warning he slipped a couple of fingers into her wet channel.

Her body bucked against his hand as her cunt exploded with an electrifying shock that made her cry out.

"You want me to stop?" he asked, evidently mistaking her response for one of pain.

"No!"

"What is your command, Annie? Do you wish me to continue?"

"Yes!" she gasped. Her heartbeat raced out of control. Her cunt drenched in fire.

Without hesitation the thumb on her passion bud began to rub harder and at the same time he began to pump his fingers violently. In and out. Deep hard strokes that left her gasping for air. Left her senses overloading between pain and desire.

Her legs trembled violently. Her pelvis arched against his plunging fingers. In moments Annie exploded in a mass of spectacular spasms that jolted her entire body.

His motions quickened.

Wantonly, she tightened her legs around his hand and rode the furious waves.

She was still trembling and breathing hard from the after-effects of her massive orgasm when he withdrew his fingers.

"There'll be more where that came from, once you release me from these restraints," he said.

Although his words were quietly spoken, Annie detected the underlying order. Detected it and reacted swiftly to his insolence.

She slapped him. Hard.

The stunned look on his face made her immediately realize her mistake. Already a red handprint appeared across his left cheek.

The stunned look shifted to one of danger. Danger and fury and betrayal. Obviously Green Eyes wasn't used to this type of harsh treatment.

She'd forgotten he wasn't a slave. He was a free male. Something unheard of these days. It would take some getting used to.

Despite the dangerous anger stiffening his muscular body, Annie's body already ached for his touch. She wanted his warm hands on her flesh. Craved his hot wet mouth on her breasts. Yearned for his massive penis to slam into her wet cunt and take her back to the heights of pleasure she'd just experienced.

The conflicting emotions of fear and sexual cravings frightened her, made her back away from him.

"I'm sorry. I...I'm not used to having a male demand something."

She wiped away the hot tears suddenly streaming down her face. She didn't know why she was overcome with such wicked emotions. One minute she was writhing from his pleasurable touch and the next minute she was crying because she'd hurt him. She was beginning to feel like a nervous wreck. Losing control of her life was something she'd never expected to happen to her.

Yet only last night, she'd given in to Cath and the Queen. Allowed them free rein over her by accepting the rings.

All because she craved Green Eyes. All because they would allow her to have him for one day. Tonight Cath and the Queen would come and his new life as a slave would begin.

The thought made her sick to her stomach. She wanted him to be safe with her. Away from the Sperm Bank and the guards who loved to torment their slaves by forcing them to service them at all hours. She wanted him all to herself. So she could fuck him. Like she'd done in the clinic.

It's just…she hadn't expected him to be so demanding. And herself to be so greedy for his touch. The price had been high to get him released. Perhaps too high.

The tears rushed out of her eyes and slid down her hot cheeks.

"Annie, don't cry. I know you aren't a violent woman." He reached out to her, but she couldn't go to him. Not when she was all weepy. Women weren't supposed to seek comfort from slaves.

"You're overwhelmed. That's all. Maybe it's best if you just release me. I'll disappear. You can go back to your regular way of life."

The thought of not seeing him again made a strange compassion, an uneasy tenderness, grip her. She didn't want to lose Green Eyes. Even if it meant sharing him with the whole village.

"I can't let you go," she found herself whispering.

"Why not?"

"They'll kill you if I do."

"I'm a pretty resourceful fellow. I'll be fine. Just tell them I escaped."

"You can't escape, because of the bracelet."

Green Eyes blinked in puzzlement.

"The bracelet on your ankle. If you go further than a half mile radius of this cabin, the droids will come."

Annie wiped the tears away from her face. "The droids will come and they'll kill you. They've already been programmed."

Chapter Eight

Joe looked down at the thin gold metal bracelet fastened around his ankle. Damn! He hadn't noticed it.

Droids? Guns? Were these women capable of such technology? And yet they lived in modest homes with no electricity, no running water and no bathrooms.

Very interesting.

"These droids? What are they? What do they do?"

"They are machines. Trackers. Electronically programmed by the Queen. If you wander out of range the droids fly in and disintegrate you."

Lovely.

"How did you invent these droids?"

"They were given to us."

Now he was getting somewhere. "By whom?"

"The ancient gods."

"What are you saying? You just woke up one day and found all this technology?"

"Yes."

Joe blinked in surprise. "I was joking. Are you serious?"

"Yes, very."

"How long ago?"

She shrugged her shoulders. "Long before I was born. The Queen is the only one allowed to control these matters."

Oh boy. This was getting a little scary. What else had these women found besides guns and droids? A nuclear bomb? He'd better get the heck out of here, find his brothers and warn them that these females weren't as innocent as they appeared.

Well, maybe innocent wasn't quite the word.

"Can't this bracelet be unlocked somehow?"

Annie shook her head. "Cath has the key. And so does the Queen."

"Obviously I'm supposed to stay here. With you. Why?"

Pink color rose in her cheeks. "I'm supposed to break you in today." Her voice sounded husky and thick.

"Break me in? In what way, Annie?"

He couldn't help but to grin as she looked away from his direct gaze. Her eyes slowly traveled to his rod. The pink tip of her tongue slipped out and she licked her bottom lip. He wished she wouldn't do that. It was a sexy gesture. Too sexy for her own good. His penis hardened under her intense gaze.

Her eyes widened with lust.

"Don't hold anything back, Annie. I need to know what I'm up against."

"This cabin is where Cath trains her slaves. She has graciously given it to us so I can show you the basics of what will be expected from you."

She watched him, anxious for a reaction. He forced himself to keep his face a passive mask. She didn't need to know the full brunt of raw anger burning in his guts. The bitch named Cath didn't have a gracious bone in her body. Something else was going on here. Something that was troubling Annie.

He watched as she padded over to a door near his bed. A door he hadn't noticed before. She opened it, allowing full view of the contents.

Joe let out a slow whistle as he viewed the array of whips, chains, feathers, ball gags, dildos, double dildos and many other accessories hanging on the door. This bondage stuff had never been his cup of tea. Despite that fact, a strange zip of excitement knotted his guts and he found himself wondering what the rest of the closet contained.

"They will be coming tonight." Annie said as she wiped away the last of her tears.

Alarm zipped up his spine. "They?"

"The Queen and Cath. They will watch us...together and then they will expect you to service—"

"The hell I will!"

"You must!"

"Listen, Annie. It's been swell hanging out with you, but I'm a one-woman kind of guy. I can't perform in front of an audience. Call it stage fright. I won't do it."

"You have no choice. And you must not let them know you can speak. Under any circumstances. Never let them know you're intelligent. At the very least they'll cut out your tongue."

"What's the worst case scenario?"

"You will be killed. By your trainer."

He just had to ask, didn't he?

"You'd kill me?"

"This is our tradition."

"You didn't answer my question, Annie. Would you kill me?"

"No." Her quick whisper was reassuring to say the least.

"And when you refuse? What will happen to you?"

"We will both be killed. As we make love to each other. In front of everyone."

"What a nice way to die."

"This is not a joke!" she snapped angrily.

"You look cute when you're mad," he teased.

She said nothing as she inhaled angrily. Her full breasts pushed seductively against the tight top she wore.

Despite his need to escape this place he found himself wanting to cup her soft breasts. Wanting to bury himself inside her heated cavern. This sexual awareness for Annie might have something to do with being constantly aroused by that machine at the Sperm Bank or maybe sex drugs, but deep down he didn't really think so. He'd been sexually aware of her the instant he'd seen her standing over him in the hub's square the other day. Despite the fear of Cath that brewed in her eyes, Annie had stopped her from going at his balls with the knife.

He owed Annie. But he didn't owe her his life. He'd have to figure out a way to gain her trust so she could help him get out of here. And he'd have to do it before tonight.

"Obviously I have no choice in this liaison. But you'll have to untie my hands. My feet. I can't perform this way."

The stunned look on her pretty face made him grin.

"You agree?"

He nodded. He had one day to figure out how to get the ankle bracelet off. And then he was outta here. Queen bitch and Cath bitch be damned. Droids or no droids. He was history. Hopefully not literally.

"They'll expose you to group sex, orgies, domination, torture, orgasm denial, anal sex..." she said as she began grabbing items out of the closet.

He didn't miss the uncomfortable looking ball gag in her hand or the ball weights. A harsh looking whip was gripped in her other hand. A butt plug was already set on the night table.

Shit! Was she serious about all this stuff? Was he nuts to be getting the slightest turn-on about Annie dominating him? Despite trying to stop it, his penis was tightening, aching with need as he watched the seductive sway of Annie's behind beneath those thin see-through shorts.

Suddenly he wanted Annie beneath him. Wanted to sink into her heated cavern.

"This penis leash will be your best friend." She held up a strange looking contraption that looked much like a miniature harness. "All the male slaves wear them whenever they are taken outdoors."

Not this guy.

"Annie, when are you getting me out of these restraints?"

She stopped sorting through the closet and glanced over at him. His guts clenched at the seriousness in her voice.

"I'm not allowed to. Not until they come."

"I can't go anywhere. You said the bracelet will prevent me from escaping. I need to walk around. Go outside and breathe some fresh air. Work on a tan. Gotta look good for the ladies tonight. You're welcome to tag along. Keep an eye on me."

Hesitation nibbled along that pretty frown.

"You already know I won't hurt you. Remember I've already had a couple of chances and I didn't. Don't you trust me yet?"

What did he have to do? Throw himself in the nearest sacrificial pool? Oh boy, he hoped they didn't have one around here.

To his surprise she nodded her head yes and in a moment she was jamming the key into the other wrist cuff. It fell open.

She slid the key into his leg restraints.

Joe could barely contain himself. A minute later he was free. Well, as free as a male slave was free in this situation.

Power ripped through him and he inhaled a deep breath. Slowly, he moved his legs up and down in an effort to get the blood moving.

"Thanks, Annie. I do appreciate it."

To his surprise a warm hand slid under his armpit and she helped him into a seated position. Dizziness swept through him. He'd been expecting it from all this lying around, so he wasn't surprised. He forced himself to fight it and a minute later it dissolved.

When he climbed out of bed, he discovered he wasn't much taller than Annie. And she was still afraid of him. Proof being as she slowly backed away from him.

"You okay?" he asked.

"I'm just not used to seeing a male slave loose."

Joe grinned and reached out his hand to her. "C'mon, let's go for a walk."

A confused smile flittered across her full lips as she stared at his outstretched hand.

"Back where I come from men and women hold hands when they go for a walk. It's a sign they like each other."

"You…like me?"

"What's not to like? C'mon, place your hand in mine."

Slowly she did as he asked.

His stomach flittered happily and sparks shot through his lower belly the instant her warm trembling hand slipped against his palm. She was still afraid of him. But in time he could tame her into trusting him.

Suddenly he wished he had more than one day with Annie. Getting to know her would have been fun. Showing her Earth's traditions would be interesting. Making love to her would have been heaven.

Although the thought of fucking Annie senseless seemed to be square on his mind, he didn't have time for sex right now. He needed to keep his mind off the sex and concentrate on finding a way out of here.

When the door opened and he felt the hot sunshine heat his face, emotions wriggled through him like a black cloud. Happiness. Sadness. Fear. If he couldn't figure a way out of here today, he wouldn't be feeling sunshine on his face again.

He'd be six feet under. Cold as a slab of concrete.

Or if he somehow lived, he'd end up servicing a whole town of dominating women. Either prospect seemed very unappealing to say the least.

Like he'd just told Annie, he was a one-woman man. Always had been. If he had to die fighting for his principles, so be it. It just didn't sit well that Annie might die alongside him. He had to figure out a way for him to escape without getting her into trouble.

"This hand holding. It feels nice." Annie said as he tugged her down the steps into the small dusty clearing in front of the grey log cabin.

He gazed at her and noticed the surprise and curiosity lurking in her pretty blue eyes. Obviously she wanted to learn his traditions. And he wanted to teach her. Surely he wouldn't be breaking protocol if he just showed her a little of Earth's ways?

"Lovers have lots of traditions."

"Lovers?" she asked.

Hot blood surged in his loins at the sweet innocent way she said the word.

"Men and women who have sex with each other and like each other are called lovers."

"Are we lovers?"

Damn. How the heck did he answer that question?

"It seems we are."

"What other traditions do lovers have?"

Oh shoot. She just had to ask, didn't she? And why the heck was he suddenly feeling so damn nervous?

"Um…well…they live together, care for each other, play house…kiss…um…"

"Show me how your people kiss?"

Was she teasing him or what? By the trusting look in her eyes, she wasn't.

He turned toward her, took her other hand in his and brought her soft body against his. Her body felt warm against him. She made him feel safe and comfortable and oh so damned horny he wanted to shove his thick shaft straight into her cunt and listen to her scream with pleasure.

Oh man! Why was he reacting so strongly to a woman he hardly knew? Was it the Florence Nightingale syndrome? Or something else? Was he hot for this woman because she was *the one*?

He almost laughed out loud at that thought. Finding his soulmate light years away from Earth sounded a bit corny, didn't it?

He let go of her and slid his hands around her waist and proceeded to slowly slide them downward to cover her silky curvy ass. Pressing his fingers into her soft ass cheeks, he pulled her hard against him. She quivered violently when he pushed his rigid desire against her abdomen.

Her heart beat hard against his chest and he felt himself drowning in her sexy scent. When his head descended toward her mouth her breath hitched with a sexy mewl.

He captured her mouth in a tender kiss. Her lips melted against his. She tasted of strawberries. Sweet and delicious.

The taste of her softness set his lips on fire, set his head to spinning with a fevered passion and he couldn't resist dipping his tongue into her mouth and exploring her hot cavern.

Her hands were exploring him as well. Sliding over his tingling skin. He gasped into her mouth when her fingers came into contact with his sensitive nipples. She tweaked and pulled until pain and pleasure intermingled in a fascinating chorus.

She trembled against him when he became more aggressive. He smiled to himself at the erotic sound of her moan. When it came right down to it women were alike everywhere. Sweet and seductive and more powerful than good liquor.

It took all his effort to stop the kiss and pull away from her.

Their gazes connected and his pulse faltered. Intimacy buzzed between them. He had the sudden urge to take her right here. Right now.

"What is that called?" she breathed.

"A kiss."

"I could get used to this kiss."

It took all the strength he could muster to rip his gaze from the sensual look in her eyes and the cute way her luscious lips tilted upwards in a wanting smile.

He intertwined his fingers with hers and said, "C'mon, let's go take that walk."

Chapter Nine

They walked side by side. As equals. And it was absolutely illegal.

From as early as she could remember she'd been taught that a proper woman always walked a few steps ahead of a male. It was a sign of importance. Of dominance.

And a proper woman always led a male slave by a penis leash. If anyone saw them like this, walking side by side, no penis leash and carefree smiles on their faces, Annie knew without a doubt they would be shot on sight.

Thank heavens they were in a secluded section of the hub, miles away from the center. Surrounded by dense trees and brush that hid them from the prying eyes of the drones or any curiosity seekers.

As they walked, she couldn't deny the joy bubbling inside her.

The Queen had allowed her one day with Green Eyes. He had been the Queen's present to her for agreeing to be her newest mate.

The way his face was all lit up with boundless wonder made her realize the price she'd paid to have him with her for such a short time hadn't been too high at all.

Green Eyes was happy and seemingly content to be here with her. That's all that mattered.

The faraway sound of rushing water made her pulses pound with excitement and she tugged at him to move faster. "There's a beautiful view just up ahead. I can't wait for you to see it. It's my most favorite spot in the whole world."

"There's already a beautiful view right here in front of me." His quiet words surprised her and she glanced back at him.

His face broke into a breathtaking smile and she recognized the lusty look in his eyes. A look that seemed to be there whenever he gazed at her. She could feel the intoxicating heat pour from his body and spill against her skin. Her heart recognized his warm male scent and began to pound with anticipation.

He tried to tug her against him, but she pulled him forward.

"You won't be sorry if you wait a couple more minutes."

A few minutes later, she led him to the edge of the fern-cloaked river. Dark blue waters littered with giant grey boulders shimmered in front of them. She pointed up to her right.

He laughed with excitement when he saw the white water tumbling over a twenty-foot high rock cliff.

"It looks fantastic!" he shouted.

Before she knew what was happening he was hauling her into the dark river and toward the crashing falls.

A few minutes later, Annie was gasping as warm falls water hammered over her head and body. Slippery rocks beneath her feet made her tipsy. The undertow tried to drag her away, but Green Eyes held her tight and drew her against his hard frame. The heat of his body slammed against her skin and his breath seductively caressed her face.

Hunger was sharp in his eyes. The yearning for her was powerful somewhere else as he pushed his promising erection against her abdomen.

She noticed his hair was darker now that it was wet. It made him look more dangerous. Sexier.

"I want to make love to you. Right here. Right now! Under the waterfall! What do you say?" he shouted.

Awareness buzzed through her and her blood heated as he waited for her response. The thought of feeling his warm mouth slide over her lips again made every nerve fiber in her body suddenly feel as if it were on fire.

She nodded eagerly in agreement.

His sexy lips curled upward into that drop-dead smile and he let go of her.

Automatically she widened her legs in an effort to keep from being pulled away by the water rushing against her body. His fingers wrenched on the hem of her drenched shirt and raised it, pulling it over her head.

Throwing it in the river, he watched it swirl away with the waves. Then he snapped his gaze onto her breasts. A puzzled little frown crossed his forehead when he saw what else they'd done to her last night.

One hand reached up and he fingered the gold nipple ring on her right breast. She inhaled at the painfully pleasant sensations. A split second later his other hand shot up and with suddenly trembling fingers he stroked her left nipple ring.

"Why?" he shouted.

"Tradition!" she yelled back through the roaring cascade. She didn't want to explain. Didn't want to tell him the truth. She wanted to make love.

As if reading her mind his large hands dropped away from her breasts and he clasped the curve of her hips.

Adrenalin soared through her veins as his head lowered to her right breast. He thrust out his seductive tongue, flicking it against her straining nipple. It beaded up like a rosebud.

His breath was hot against her breast. Hot and arousing, making her soft mounds tighten and swell with anticipation.

"You taste delicious!" he growled. "Damned delicious."

Her blood pumped hot through her veins as his blistering mouth covered her nipple. His teeth pinched at the nipple ring until her rosy tip ached. Tremors coursed through her body as he did the same to her other nipple. When he was finished, he pulled away and admired his work.

Her nipples stood to attention under his caressing stare. Two hard stiff trembling peaks. He smiled with satisfaction and cupped both sides of her face. His mouth came down on hers.

Hot desire exploded in her cunt as his tongue probed into her mouth.

He tore at her shorts as he kissed her. She managed to step out of them and imagined her pants joining her shirt in the massive whirlpools below.

Suddenly he broke the kiss, leaving her mouth swollen and trembling. Leaving her mind swirling from the sweet pleasure.

Swooping down he captured her left nipple with the wet heat of his mouth once again. This time he was rougher. More demanding.

His seductive tongue circled her trembling nipple like a vulture. His teeth pulled gently on her nipple ring causing a friction of blinding ecstasy. He attacked her other breast with the same zeal.

Prodding. Poking. Sucking. Biting. He kept attacking her until she was writhing against the onslaught from the tension zinging through her cunt. Tension and hunger. It made her mad with want. Made her want him inside her.

"Now, Green Eyes," she whispered.

He must have heard the plea in her voice for he stopped his ministrations on her breast, pulled away and grinned.

"I want you to call me by my real name. Call me Joe."

"Joe?" Instantly she liked the name, but she would like it even better if he would hurry up and fuck her.

"Say it again."

"Joe."

"Again."

"Joe."

"Say, I love you, Joe."

Annie blinked in surprise. Her heart raced with strange emotions she'd never felt before.

Love? She remembered her teacher talking about love in the history classes. It was said to be an affection between a woman and her male. A word the male used to dominate the woman into doing whatever he wanted to her.

Confusion and anticipation ripped her apart. Did she want to be dominated by this male? The answer came quickly.

Yes, she wanted Joe. She wanted him with all her heart. And she'd do anything for him. Anything!

"I love you, Joe."

Although the words were a mere whisper, they sounded like a shout as they curled through the crashing waterfall.

His green eyes sparkled proudly at her answer and his large hands curled over the curve of her hips sending fire ripping through her very core.

"I love you too, Annie. Damn it! I do love you." He said it as if he'd just realized the fact.

And then he laughed. The sound came from deep within his chest. A wonderful seductive sound that sent chills of joy cascading through her.

His hot slippery hands slid over her hips to cup her bare ass cheeks and he swept her into his embrace. When she felt his naked shaft press hard against the door of her vagina she wanted him to penetrate her. To take her and quench the fire that burned her body.

Instead, he kissed her. Hard. With so much emotion that the fierceness of his lips pressing against her stole her breath from her lungs and shocked her brain.

She'd just told a slave she loved him. How could this be? How had he changed her whole life in such a short time?

He was a dangerous male. Exciting. Addictive. Like a drug. And she wanted him all to herself. She would die fighting to protect him from their plans.

The last thought startled her and then the realization sank deep into her brain. Yes, she would die fighting for him...

A hot thumb slammed against her pleasure nub making her hips arch into his hand. He began to rub furiously until her cries ripped free from her mouth and into his. He rubbed so hard the pleasure became unbearable and her body exploded in convulsions.

His finger fell away and his thick penis entered her wet cunt in one swift deep stroke, surprising her with its killing pleasure. His quick thrust threw her off guard. Obliterated all sane thoughts.

The rocks beneath her feet shook as he withdrew and pounded into her again.

And again.

Her body bucked against his, welcoming his wild delicious strokes. Violent tremors laced through her. She ripped her mouth away, gasping madly for air. Stars danced behind her eyes as a splintering orgasm ripped her body apart, turning her legs to jelly.

Grabbing his powerful shoulders for support, Annie held on tight as he continued to thrust his huge cock into her. The scent of their lovemaking filled the air. The sucking sound of his solid thrusts was like music to her ears.

She came again, her body convulsing wildly. The excruciating pleasure made her scream and the roaring water carried the sound downstream.

She could see his teeth were gritted with determination, the corded muscles in his neck thick and pulsing as he continued to fuck her. Yet during all this time he somehow maintained eye contact. It was as if he couldn't get enough of looking at her. As if he wanted to see the pleasure enveloping her face.

When he noticed she was watching him, he fucked her harder until she closed her eyes and screamed from the ecstasy.

The man was an animal the way he pumped into her. Hard and primal and oh so deliciously good.

He drove her toward yet another orgasm. When she began to come down from it, she could hear Joe's ragged hiss as he shot his hot seed deep into her.

Chapter Ten

Joe Hero had never been in love before. Didn't have anything to compare to this insane attraction he felt for Annie. Actually it was more than attraction.

Under the waterfall when he'd made love to her, he hadn't been able to tear his eyes from her face. As he'd looked at the ecstasy shining there, something had just snapped inside him. Suddenly he'd realized he couldn't live without her warm soft body pressed against his. Couldn't live without hearing her sweet voice whisper, "I love you".

She was a beautiful woman who wanted to be loved. And he wanted to be the one to do the loving.

"What are you thinking, Joe?" she asked as she snuggled closer to him.

With one finger she drew lazy circles around his left nipple and he sucked in his breath at the pleasure she caused. He could lie here in the soft bed of ferns all day. Stare at the waterfall gushing like a thick silver ribbon into the river and make love to Annie over and over again. Just like he had been doing.

He couldn't get enough of her. Couldn't seem to stop himself from plunging his aching shaft into her succulent cunt. She was as addictive to him as a junkie was addicted to heroin.

Most of the day had disappeared and he hadn't even tried to look for a way out. Maybe because deep down, he knew there was no way out. He was in love with Annie. Whatever she wanted him to do, he'd do it, maybe even stay here…

"I was thinking of how nice it would be having you wake up next to me every morning," he whispered against her ear.

Her finger stopped circling. "That's not possible."

"If I stay, can't we work something out with Cath and this Queen of yours?"

"The deal has already been made. It can't be changed." The finality in her voice made him realize she was telling the truth. Something had been forged between the three women. And it involved him.

"What was the deal between you, Cath and the Queen?"

"I don't want to talk about it with you."

"Why not? If it involves me—"

She looked up into his eyes. He saw confusion there. Confusion and pain.

His protective instincts kicked in. Something was terribly wrong.

"I want you to leave with me."

She didn't answer.

Fear blossomed in his chest. "I know this is too fast. What I'm asking of you is something you should think about for awhile, but we don't have time. I don't want to leave you behind when I go. I won't. "

"I told you, you can't escape. It's not possible."

Desperation slammed into his guts.

"Anything is possible, Annie, when you set your mind to it."

"You don't seem to understand what's happening here, Joe. You're very...well endowed. The women want you. You don't know what I had to do just to get one day with you."

"What did you have to do, Annie?"

She didn't look at him. Instead she traced another lazy circle around his nipple. "You only need to know that the women want you. Bad."

"And what about you, Annie? Do you want me?"

"Yes."

"How bad?"

She didn't answer.

"Not bad enough to help me escape?"

Her lush body stiffened against him. He realized immediately he'd said the wrong thing.

"Is that what this is about? You're having sex with me to soften me up? To use me? To get me to help you escape?"

"I'm sorry, I shouldn't have said that. It wasn't fair."

"If you hadn't said it, you'd be thinking it, Green Eyes."

"What do you want me to do, Annie? Do you want me to stay? I will if you want me to. I will fuck all those women just so I can be with you."

He'd never been one to scare easily in his lifetime. That's why he'd been so laid back about getting caught by a handful of naked women. He'd figured he'd find a way out of this problem somehow. But now as he saw the tears shine in Annie's eyes, he was suddenly scared. Very scared he would lose her.

"After today, we can never be together. Ever."

Her words crushed him. Made his head spin. "Why not?"

"Because of the Queen. It's tradition she can only have sex with females. She's had her eye on me for quite some time. The other day she approached me. Her female mate is Cath and they decided they want more spice in their sex life. They want me as their next mate. I will only have sex with the two of them and any other females the Queen decides to bring into the arrangement."

Joe's mind whirled. The Queen and Cath wanted Annie for themselves? They wanted to fuck Annie?

"That was the agreement you made? You agreed to have sex with them? Just to be with me? God, Annie, why the hell did you do that?"

The tears in her eyes overflowed and Joe reached out to her. She rolled away from him and sat up. Her bare breasts heaved as she inhaled a sob.

"Don't touch me, Green Eyes. It's over. Tonight, we will have sex and they will evaluate how you perform. Cath will begin to train you…and I'll be going with the Queen. She's promised me that I can get the job I've always wanted."

"What job?"

"Helping the women in the Breeding Prison give birth. The doctor they have right now is almost ready to be put down."

Joe inhaled sharply. "What do you mean put down?"

"She's going into menopause. When that happens she will be killed. Just like all of us when our time comes."

"But why kill you when you reach menopause?"

"Because we will have outgrown our usefulness."

"I don't understand."

"Our hubs are kept alive by producing a certain amount of female and male children. These children are produced in the prison system. If a woman breaks the law she is sent to prison. Our sentences are based on the number of children she must produce. If she can't produce any children, there is no sentence available for her, so she's useless."

Joe closed his eyes and shook his head. This couldn't be happening. It was like something out of science fiction. Like the ancient movie *Logan's Run.* People being executed once they reached a certain age, or in this case, menopause. It was obscene.

"This is crazy! You are not going to be fucked by some damn Queen. Not if I can help it. And no one's going to kill you when your time comes."

"It's too late. I've already accepted the rings."

"The clit and nipple rings?"

"It's our tradition. When a female becomes a mate of the Queen, she must accept the rings. I already went through the ceremony. After the ceremony the new mate is blessed by the Queen with whatever presents she wishes. I asked for my dream job and for you. But the Queen only agreed to allow me one day with you."

"I'm a free man. She doesn't have the right to give me to you. I made love to you of my own free will. And I sure as hell won't let you go to the Queen."

"I gave her my word!"

"Then undo your damn word!"

"You don't have a say. You're a captive of the Queen now. A slave! You have no rights!" Hysteria edged her voice.

Before Joe could stop her, Annie stood and looked down at him. She placed her hand over her left breast, covering her heart.

"I will keep today in my heart forever, Joe. It was magical. Never in my wildest dreams did I think I would ever experience something so beautiful, but it's over. We have to return to reality. I'm going back to the cabin. Please don't try to escape."

Joe watched in stunned numbness as she padded naked through the tall ferns and disappeared into the forest. He clenched his jaw in frustration as something tight clamped around his heart. She'd sacrificed herself to the Queen so she could have a day with him? He didn't know what to make of it. Didn't know what he should be feeling.

He did feel numb. Shocked. He didn't understand the need for Annie to have to bow to the Queen to get her dream job. Sleeping with the boss to get a promotion. It was akin to sexual assault back on Earth. Evidently here on Paradise things were different.

He wished his logical scientific mind would take over. Wished he could make himself separate his emotions and put Annie into the same category as the other women on this planet. But Annie wasn't like the other women. She was different. He'd known it the instant he'd first seen her. The instant she'd made love to him in the clinic. Oh boy, he had it bad for her.

His gaze fell back to the ankle bracelet. He didn't know why he'd offered to stay here and service a whole town of women just to be with Annie.

Temporary insanity.

He was a man who needed his freedom. Needed to make his own decisions. And he needed to get the hell out of here.

By the looks of the setting sun, he didn't have much time left.

* * * * *

The instant Green Eyes was out of earshot, Annie allowed the sorrow to fill her heart. Tears blinded her as she stumbled along the trail.

His comment about her loving him enough to help him escape had angered her and she'd lashed out, trying to cut all ties with Green Eyes.

It had hurt to see the utter look of devastation shadow his face. It hurt so bad she thought her whole body would explode into tiny splinters.

But his words of love were just that. Words. Words he'd used to get what he wanted from her.

She shook her head in denial. Deep in her heart she knew it wasn't true. He did have serious feelings about her. She'd seen the emotions churning in his eyes. Felt it in the possessive way he touched her. The way he'd made love to her…

He hadn't fucked her. He had made love to her.

It had been in the gentle way his hands had caressed her body. The way concern had ripped through his eyes when he'd seen her nipple rings.

Annie wiped the tears away from her eyes and chuckled to herself as everything suddenly made sense. What they had together had been more than physical. She knew that now. She must have known it too when she'd made love to him that first time in the clinic. It had surfaced in the way she'd ached to set him free.

Heck, something had clicked into place the first time she'd looked into his eyes and seen the intelligence brewing there.

Oh God! What was she going to do? How was she going to help Green Eyes?

Anything is possible, once you set your mind to it.

Joe had said those words not more than a few minutes ago.

Hope soared in her heart. She would have to think of a way to help him. Hopefully an answer would come to her.

Her mind was still searching for answers to find a way to help Joe when a few moments later Annie opened the door to her cabin and stepped inside.

"Hello Annie."

Annie froze as the young Queen's seductive voice curled through the room.

She lay on the bed. Long muscular legs spread wide open. Her shaved pussy exposed and eagerly waiting for her.

Chapter Eleven

"Where's my slave, Annie?"

Annie cringed at the harsh sound of Cath's voice as she stepped out from behind the open door.

Oh God! They were already here!

When she saw the two giant black double ended dildos in Cath's hands, her legs began to tremble.

"You're early," Annie whispered.

"Where the fuck is my slave?" Cath shouted.

"I'm right here."

Annie jumped at the harshness in Joe's voice as he stepped through the open doorway behind her.

Both the Queen and Cath froze, their eyes wide with shock. Obviously they were having the same reaction as she had when she'd found out Joe could speak more than a few words.

He didn't waste any time taking advantage of the situation. Grabbing Cath, he wrapped a muscular arm around her neck. For a moment, Annie thought Joe might choke her, but he didn't.

Cath looked horrified. Pale. As if she were about to faint right on the spot.

Annie could only imagine the fear coursing through Cath's veins as she most likely thought there was another Slave Uprising going on.

"Where's the key for the ankle bracelet, ladies?" he demanded.

Cath, too stunned to speak, could only shake her head in disbelief.

"You!" He nodded toward the naked Queen. "Are you the Queen?"

"I am. My name is Jacey."

To Annie's surprise the Queen's voice sounded dangerously calm, despite her pale face.

"Where's the key to the ankle bracelet?"

"He can speak? How is this possible?" she asked Annie.

"The key!" Joe's shout made both Annie and Cath jump. But the Queen remained unmoved. Her eyes narrowed with curiosity as she studied Joe.

"Who are you? Who educated you? Where did you come from?"

"Listen, lady. This is no time to break out the tea and biscuits and chat. I asked you a question."

"And if I don't give you the key?"

"Then I break your lady's neck. And I'll enjoy doing it."

"And I'll enjoy watching."

At her answer a frightened whimper escaped Cath's lips.

The Queen casually slid her legs together, then slowly got off the bed. Her wide hips sashayed and her heavy breasts swayed as she padded toward Joe.

"Easy does it. Don't try anything funny," he warned.

The Queen smiled seductively and stopped. "I've read about men like you in the Ancient Books. Talking men who demand. Fight. And kill. For no reason at all. For nothing more than…for sport."

"Sounds a lot like the way you run this place, Jacey. Now about the key?"

"She keeps it in her belly bag," Annie said. Ignoring the Queen's surprised look, she gazed around the room for the item and saw it hanging on a nearby hook.

"Get it, Annie," Joe ordered.

Annie bristled at his command. The urge to slap him was strong but she caught herself.

He was a free man. Not a slave. She needed to remember that.

Rushing over to the bag, she reached into it. When the cool metal of the key touched her fingertips, Annie sighed in relief.

"Get the cuff off, Annie."

Another order.

Annie prickled.

The Queen tilted her head in curiosity as she watched Annie.

But Annie knew she had to do as Joe said. She wanted him free.

"Think what you're about to do, Annie. Think real hard," the Queen warned. "You're endangering your career possibilities by holding that key in your hand. If you go any further…"

Her stern words dangled over Annie's head as if it were a sharp blade ready to slice through her neck.

Annie stopped dead in her tracks.

Joe cursed beneath his breath.

The Queen was right. Helping Joe escape would be the end of her life here at the Hub. Her dreams of delivering babies at the Prison would be dead.

But what about Joe? It wasn't right to hold him here against his will. If she asked him to stay, he'd die inside. One day at a time. She knew it. She'd feel the same way if she were imprisoned and forced to do what they were planning to do to him.

Annie took a step forward.

"Annie, I gave you those rings for a reason." Annie heard Joe's angry inhalation at the Queen's soft spoken words.

"I granted you one day with the slave at your request because I sensed how much you wanted him. I was taking a huge risk by allowing this. You know it goes against tradition, Annie. Once you agree to be mine, you are mine, until I say otherwise. I thought you understood that. If you put the key back into my bag, we'll never speak of this again. But you'll have to do it now."

"I'm sorry, Jacey. We have to set him free."

The look of hurt in the Queen's eyes sent a shiver of guilt through Annie. She was denying the Queen. She was severing all ties with her own world.

She had thought she would be devastated at leaving her dreams behind.

Strangely enough, she wasn't.

Though she was frightened. Terrified of the unknown.

"You let him go and we might be facing another Slave Uprising in the not so distant future," the Queen said. "Remember what happened the last time?"

Annie shivered at the Queen's cold words but forced herself to slide the key into Joe's ankle bracelet. It opened immediately.

"Put it on Cath's ankle," Joe ordered.

Annie did as she was instructed.

"I'm leaving. Will you come with me?" he said to her.

Cath's eyes widened in shock at Joe's question. The Queen frowned.

"I'll throw some food together."

With trembling hands she grabbed a sack and began tossing food into it.

"You can't be serious, Annie!" Cath had finally found her tongue. "Where will you go? He's a slave. A beast. Dammit! This is treason. You'll be hunted down alongside him. You'll end up in the Breeding Prison, getting fucked by a machine and producing slaves for the rest of your life! Is that what you want, Annie?"

Her whole body was trembling by the time she joined Joe at the door. Power intermingled with confusion as Joe slipped his hand around hers.

She was doing the right thing, wasn't she?

"I'll be with Joe. That's all that matters."

"You won't get far," the Queen warned. "My women will hunt you down before you get a mile away from here."

To Annie's surprise Joe let Cath loose and pushed her away from him. She stumbled against the counter, gasping and holding her hand to her bruised neck.

Grabbing the bag of food from Annie, he nodded to the open doorway. "Let's go!"

And before she knew what was happening he was tugging her through the open doorway and into the looming darkness.

Annie dared one last peek over her shoulder as they raced down the steps. One last peek at the only life she had known.

The Queen stood there in the doorway. Stood straight and proud. Annie had expected to see anger plastered across her. Anger, fury and betrayal. She saw none of that.

All she saw was the look of envy twinkling in her eyes.

But that had to be Annie's imagination.

Chapter Twelve

Annie was tiring. Joe could hear it in her frantic gasps for air. Could feel it in the way she stumbled behind him. He was practically dragging her now as they burst through the tree line, their legs snarling with the tall ferns as they crashed through them and ran onto the sharp rocks at the river's edge.

She'd fallen a few times since they'd escaped. But he never let go of her. If he did, he had the feeling she'd somehow disappear into the night and he'd never see her again.

His own lungs burned. Pinpricks of pain cut into his naked feet as he climbed over the jagged rocks. His limbs were afire with the need to rest.

Behind them came the women's excited screams. The hunt was on and they were closing in fast.

Annie shouted for him to stop. She was at the end of her rope. And so was he.

In the moonlight he watched her breasts heave wildly with every tortured breath. Saw the way her eyes were scrunched tight as she sucked in the cool night air.

"We have to keep moving," he urged.

"Can't! Need a break!"

Try as he might, he couldn't bring himself to tug on her and start running again.

Instead she plopped onto a nearby boulder, pulling him down beside her. Her head lolled forward and she sighed in defeat.

From behind them, the wild whoops of the women grew louder. Joe stiffened as the eerie sounds knifed through his body. The women were mad. Frenzied. Like sharks smelling blood as they honed in on their prey.

Damn! Why had he let Annie help him? Why the hell hadn't he just pretended to go insane and attack all three women instead of being friendly with Annie?

Hindsight was twenty-twenty. The damage was done. Because of his stupidity Annie would pay. She'd end up just like those other women he'd seen in the Sperm Bank section of the prison. She'd be strapped down to one of those merciless machines while the guards watched and laughed.

Joe closed his eyes. What the hell kind of world was this? A world where women treated their own with such violence. Sentencing them to producing children in prison simply because they'd done something wrong.

He remembered the blond woman named Virgin. Recalled how the hatred had shattered her pretty face when she'd been told she would have to bear another male child. She'd been horrified at that thought. He wondered if she would hurt herself or the baby.

Joe caught himself. Shit! Their baby.

How many women had been impregnated by his sperm? How many of his male offspring would be subjected to this degrading world? His daughters made to fuck the Queen, like Annie was supposed to do.

Joe shivered as he remembered the two giant black double ended dildos in Cath's hand. Cath and the Queen had obviously been expecting Annie to participate in something with them. He'd seen the teasing smile on Cath's face as she'd held the dildos out to Annie. Seen the wetness between the Queen's legs as she'd lain on the bed, her legs wide open waiting for Annie to join her.

God! What Annie must have agreed to do with them just because she'd wanted a day with him and her dream job.

Joe opened his eyes and he saw a flicker of light just beyond the jungle line.

His heart sank.

A torch.

The women were coming. In a matter of moments, they'd be discovered and the horrors would begin.

"The river!" Annie gasped. "Into the river! They can't follow our tracks. We'll go upstream."

Joe nodded. Why the hell hadn't he thought of that?

Grabbing her hand, he slung the food bag over his shoulder and both rushed into the cool water.

A heavy current whipped against Joe's torso as he pulled Annie's smaller frame upstream with him. It was hard going. One wrong slip with a foot and they'd both be plunging into the churning waters and carried away. Most likely drown if the women didn't catch them first.

They had just snuggled into a dark bend in the river, when Joe spotted the handful of women holding torches rush onto the same shore they'd rested on only moments earlier.

His heart crashed against his chest. Beside him, Annie shivered and her teeth chattered violently. So loud he hoped the newcomers couldn't hear it above the rushing sound of the water.

One of the women pointed downstream and in one solid mass, they splashed into the water with violent screams and whistles. They disappeared down the river.

A moment later another group emerged from the forest. This time there were at least a dozen women. Joe recognized the naked leader's voluptuous body. The Queen.

Beside him, Annie leaned into him, trying to bury herself against his frame.

Joe's heart picked up speed as the Queen's gaze raked along the river where the other women had vanished. Her narrowed eyes scanned every rock and crevice. When she saw nothing downstream, she turned her head in their direction.

Annie's breath hitched. He sensed her fear and he held her hand tight in case she decided to bolt.

For the longest time the Queen stared directly at them.

A horrible sinking feeling hit Joe deep in his gut as an odd smile curled her lips. If he didn't know any better he'd swear the Queen knew they were here. Suddenly she turned her head and pointed downstream. In a flutter, all the women scrambled into a single file and headed down the river.

Joe exhaled a heavy sigh of relief. The Queen had let them go. Why? And how had she known they were here?

His answer came fast. From the corner of his eye he saw the metallic glints shine off Annie's breasts. Shit! The moonlight had reflected off her nipple rings.

"She saw us," he whispered.

"The Queen? That's not possible. She would have sent the women after us."

Joe shook his head slowly. "She definitely saw us. What I want to know is why she's letting us go?"

"Maybe she decided I was right? Maybe she realized you should be free?"

Uneasiness churned through Joe. "I think she's up to something."

"What?"

"I don't know. Maybe they're swinging back up along the trees. Coming in from behind us. Taking us by surprise."

"Whether she is or not, we have to leave," Annie whispered.

"The only way is upstream. But if the Queen decides to come after us we won't get far in this current."

"There may be another way. We head up as far as the falls. Just above it is another river. If we stay in the river we won't leave tracks. They'll have to split up if they come this way."

"How many rivers run through this area?"

"Three."

Joe's stomach sank. So much for trying to find out which river he'd been at when he'd been shot. It would take too long to search for the right river. Too long to try and locate his equipment and food.

There was only one choice left.

"I need to get to the sea."

"Freedom Sea?"

"That's where my brothers are." And the spaceship, he added silently. Hopefully they hadn't been captured and had just gotten lost and found their way back to the ship and were leisurely sipping some ice-cold beer, lounging on the beach, waiting for him to return.

"Brothers?"

"Two more males, like me."

"There are more of you?" She gasped in shock.

"Just two more. Don't worry, they won't hurt you. I promise."

She nodded, but he could see the worry lurking in her eyes.

"The river above the falls will lead us to the parallel river. The other river goes through the hunt camp. From the camp a trail will lead directly to Freedom Sea."

"How far away is this parallel river from this one?"

"Twenty or so miles east over land. Longer if we follow the waterways."

"I remember coming to at one point and the women were talking about a hunt camp. There was one giant tree in a meadow. With a river running right by it. Is that the hunt camp you mentioned?"

Annie nodded. "It's where..." She bit her bottom lip.

"Where you bring your male slaves after you've captured them."

"Yes. But I've only been there once. When I had to catch and bed my first male."

"A little too much information, thanks," he grumbled.

In the moonlight he caught a flash of her white teeth as she smiled. "You don't like to hear that, do you?"

Joe shrugged. "I think it's best if we discuss this another time, don't you?"

"Time to move?"

"Time to move," he agreed.

Making sure no one was watching, Joe and Annie left the tiny cove and headed upstream.

Chapter Thirteen

They traveled all night with numerous short breaks. As they'd passed the fern bed where they'd made love, Annie had yearned to lie down there and sleep. Or better yet lie down and cover Joe's body with her own. To make love to him like there was no tomorrow.

And since there might not be a tomorrow for either of them, she tried hard to keep up to Joe's punishing gait.

Pain was her constant companion as she splashed through the river. She hurt everywhere. Her feet ached from the rugged rocks on the riverbed. Her knees and elbows were scraped raw from the falls she'd taken. But most of all her heart ached for Joe.

Determination etched his features. She hoped he still wasn't weak from his neck wound. Although it did look as if it was already healed nicely, thanks to the Quick Healing injection she'd given him. Hopefully his days of being held captive at the Sperm Bank hadn't drained him of his much-needed energy.

Annie couldn't help but to smile at the last thought.

No, he possessed energy. Lots of it. He'd kept up with her intense lovemaking. He'd allowed her full rein as she'd lain or sat on top of him for more times than she could count. But she hadn't been able to get enough of his delightful kisses. Or of his massive penis as she'd sunk onto him.

Finally the yellow streaks of sunlight filtered their way through the jungle trees. The hunt camp was only a few minutes ahead but what she saw circling in the sky made her blood run cold.

Annie ordered Joe to stop.

"Vultures." She breathed and pointed to the ugly birds spinning above their heads. "Someone must be using the camp. Most likely the Yellow Hairs."

"The Yellow Hairs?"

"They're our closest neighbors. Ten miles to the east. That would explain the vultures."

Joe cocked a curious eyebrow. "Dare I ask?"

"The Yellow Hairs are a violent hub. Cannibals. They eat many of the males they catch and they don't associate with us because of our brown hair."

"You're kidding."

"I'm serious. Only yellow hairs are allowed to join that hub."

"Interesting. Women grouped by hair color. I guess I got lucky with the brunettes." He grinned and reached out to sift a stray strand of her hair through his fingers.

His muscular power washed over her in hot waves. His male scent made her heart pound harder. Made her cunt go wet with need.

He let go of her hair. "Maybe we should rest for awhile."

"We can stay here until the vultures descend. When they do, it'll mean the camp is empty. There's a small cellar there. We should find some food. It is the way of women to always leave extra food for whoever comes next."

"As long as it ain't any body parts." Joe grumbled.

Annie couldn't help but laugh.

"Speaking of food. Let's go and sit on the bank. I'm starving," she said.

They nestled on a large flat moss-covered rock hidden from the river. Facing each other they sat and ate in silence. Both listened to the waves slapping against the rocky shoreline and remained alert for any new sounds that might tip them off that someone could be following.

Her homemade bread had never tasted so delicious and the raisins she'd brought along were the sweetest she'd ever had.

After finishing his meager meal Joe reached out and curled his fingers around her ankle. His touch was electrifying. The look of concern in his eyes made her heart suspend in her chest and she wanted to wrap her arms around his neck and tell him she was fine.

"Does it hurt bad?" he asked. His warm fingers whispered over the raw cuts on the soles of her cold feet giving her a savage need to feel his hands on the rest of her body.

"It's nothing I can't handle," she reassured him.

Her breathing grew shallow with his caresses and his sexy scent made her dizzy with desire.

"What about you?" she asked.

"Nothing that can't wait."

His kissable lips suddenly curled upward into a breath-sucking grin. Her heart gave a sudden lurch at the sight.

"Well, there is something that can't wait."

He lowered her foot and reached out. She moaned as the provocative heat of his hands cupped both her breasts, his touch burning through her skin, making her shiver with an untamed pleasure.

"We really should save our energy," she found herself saying.

His eyes darkened with desire.

Fiery heat began to build in her lower belly.

"I agree, but if they catch us we won't be able to make love to each other. So I'm game to take advantage of our free time."

He leaned closer, his hot cheek touching the side of her face. The stubble on his face brushing sparks of pleasure along the curve of her jaw.

To her surprise he nibbled on her earlobe. The intimate gesture made her senses grow sharper. Made her want him to plunge his hot shaft deep inside her.

"Is this ear nibbling another one of your traditions?" She giggled.

"Uh huh."

His callused hands began to knead her breasts, making them feel fuller. Making them tingle with need.

"Every time I look at you naked, I want you beneath me."

Annie froze at his words.

"Beneath you? It's against our laws. The woman is always on top. It is our sign that we dominate males."

The sexy nibbling on her ear stopped. "Where I come from, males and females are equals. We do it in all kinds of positions."

"What…what kind of positions?"

"I can show you."

He could show her? Sweet heavens, no. She couldn't allow him to show her. A proper woman never allowed the male full rein.

As if sensing her inner turmoil, he lifted her head and grinned at her.

"You look properly shocked."

"We've been taught women on top of the male. I...I've never done it any other way except standing under the waterfall, with you."

And she'd loved it!

"Honey, you don't know what you've been missing. We have many, many different positions. The possibilities are endless. We do it with the woman on top. Standing. Man on top. Rear entry standing up...many others ways. For instance in the ass..."

In her ass? By a male? How interesting.

"Which is your favorite position?" she found herself asking.

"All of them."

"Teach them to me." She couldn't believe she'd just said that.

"I thought you said we should save our energy?"

"We can rest later."

Her hand lifted and she ran a finger along the hot edges of his lips. Suddenly she wanted him to try out every position he knew.

"Start with the one at the top of your favorite list," she suggested.

Joe shifted beside her and Annie caught a glimpse of his massive penis, already hard and eager for her.

"You can tell me to stop any time you don't feel comfortable," he whispered.

Annie nodded. Fire danced through her veins and her heart cracked like a jackhammer as he slowly knelt down in front of her.

"Lie down on your back and spread your legs," he instructed softly.

She did as he suggested, stretching out on the warm softness of the moss. She watched with curiosity as he grabbed the food sack, emptied the meager contents beside them. Scrunching up the bag, he gently stuffed it under her hips, bringing her cunt up toward him.

He stared down into her face, his eyes deadly serious.

"I won't hurt you, Annie."

"I know you won't. I trust you." And she did.

Her cunt burned with want as he took his thick pulsing penis in his hand and lowered it between her thighs.

She wasn't surprised to find that his hot male flesh slid easily into her. She was wet for him. She was always wet for him.

His pulsing rod was hot and her vaginal muscles welcomed him eagerly, clamping around his male flesh as he entered.

To her surprise he hooked his hands beneath her knees and hoisted her ankles over his shoulders. She gasped as his calloused hands slid off her legs and cradled her ass cheeks. Sensations ripped through her as he thrust his strong erection fiercely into her very core, filling her completely.

His smile was bright and sweet as he grinned down at her.

"You like?"

"Don't stop!" she gasped.

"This is one of the positions best to hit a woman's G-spot."

She didn't really care what a G-spot was. All she knew was she wanted to cry out at the lovely pressure building inside her vagina as he began to rock back and forth. His rapid thrusts were deep and powerful and they increased the fantastic pressure building inside her lower belly.

Within moments a fierce spasm ripped through her cunt and she moaned shamelessly.

She heard Joe's ragged uneven breath as his fierce strokes grew faster, more demanding, more animalistic.

Closing her eyes she allowed her cunt to contract around his hard penis, her body exploding in a river of spasms. Each spasm was more powerful than the last.

His penis kept plunging harder and she shuddered as the violent waves engulfed her. The intensity of the pleasure took hold of her and Annie rode the searing waves into a blinding madness.

She cried out again and again as the powerful orgasms hit, not caring if anyone heard her. Her mind was gone, her body enveloped in the intense bliss her male was creating as he hammered his thick rod into her cunt.

He stretched her insides as he continued to plunge ruthlessly, making tears of joy stream down her cheeks.

And soon her cries were drowned out by his heavy groans as he joined her in her world of ecstasy.

More shudders ripped through her, sending her spinning through the madness of pleasure. Spasms of agonizing pleasure, they engulfed her and Annie cried out again and again until she was finally spent.

That's when Joe came. Hard. His hot seed spilling into her like a tidal wave.

Annie smiled as his completion filled her and dripped out of her cunt, drenching the insides of her thighs.

She smiled and thanked the Goddess of Freedom for sending her this male. A male who could make her wildest dreams come true.

Chapter Fourteen

Joe awoke to sunshine slicing straight into his eyes. His body ached and he felt as if a hundred women had beaten every part of him. Groaning he lifted a hand to keep the sun out of his eyes. From beside him he heard a sweet giggle. Turning his head he smiled at Annie, who propped herself up on an elbow.

She was watching him. Her cheeks were flushed from their intense lovemaking. Her cute lips twitched as she tried to hide another giggle.

"Did I hurt you?" she asked.

"Actually I should be asking you that question with all your moans and cries."

She hid a smile and shrugged her shoulders. Her luscious breasts bounced at the gesture and he felt himself harden again. It took all his strength to keep from reaching out and dragging her on top of him.

"What can I say? You bring out the best in me."

"I'm glad you enjoyed it."

The rosy shade in her cheeks increased a notch. "How about you? Did you enjoy it?"

"Immensely. You are the most beautiful woman I have ever had the pleasure of fucking."

"Does this mean there have been others?"

"A few, but they always left me wanting something more."

"They didn't satisfy you?"

"I guess when it came right down to it, no, they were lacking something. And you? What about your males, did they satisfy you?"

"They were passable enough. Unfortunately I haven't had a male since the Slave Uprising last year."

Well, that explained her desire for sex at every turn. He inhaled sharply as she skimmed a hot finger down the length of his neck and over his chest muscles.

"I've been meaning to ask you about the Slave Uprising. How did that happen?"

"The male slaves took over the brothel town. It is co-owned by the Yellow Hairs and us."

"Really? Your hub went into business with them? Despite your differences?"

"It was a lucrative investment until the Uprising. Unfortunately many of the women were…taken against their will. It is our law that only prisoners be allowed to give birth and so when the slaves impregnated free females…it wasn't a very good time for our hub. The Queen decided to ban our females from going to the brothels. She still hasn't removed the ban."

"Why did the slaves revolt in the first place?"

She ran a teasing finger over his stomach and Joe couldn't help but to suck in a heated breath.

"Ah, that's a long story. But the short of it is a Yellow Hair broke the law and decided to educate a male she favored in the brothel. He in turn educated the other males in secret. The slaves then decided they didn't want to serve the females anymore, they wanted it to be the other way around. They took the town and they fucked many of the free females…fortunately the women were able to fight back and regained the hub."

A shiver of fear ripped up Joe's spine. "What happened to you? Did they…?"

"I was lucky to have not been visiting the brothel town at the time. I was unharmed."

"So, what happened to everyone? The slaves? And the female who started everything."

"Most of the educated males were executed by the Yellow Hairs. The rest escaped, including the female and her male. But the female was eventually captured. She is in the prison. She's had one male child already."

His body tensed at the thought of the women he'd seen hooked up to the fucking machines. Most hadn't wanted the experience but once they'd been hooked to it, the agonizing ecstasy had changed their minds.

As if sensing she was losing him, Annie's scorching finger dipped into his belly button.

Damned if that didn't turn him on hotter than an inferno. He couldn't help but to reach out and take her into his arms, cradling her soft body against him.

She giggled mischievously and he realized this had been her plan all along. To get him aroused.

"Don't you ever get tired?" He laughed.

"When I see you naked, I want to make love to you."

Joe grinned as he heard almost the exact words he'd said to her earlier.

"I've been using my imagination about these positions you were talking about. I want you to take me from the rear," she whispered against his neck.

Her words incited an aching desire deep in his gut.

Burying his nose into her silky hair, he inhaled the earthy scent of her. The woman was heaven sent. She wanted sex all the time. As if he were a chunk of sweet candy she couldn't get enough of.

"From behind it is," he agreed.

Eagerly she broke their embrace and kneeled on all fours, sticking her beautifully rounded ass up in the air toward him.

He didn't waste any time placing his legs inside hers and grabbing her soft hips with his hands. Her body was hot beneath him and she trembled with excitement. Holding her steady he slowly entered her and watched in stunned fascination as his thick pulsing penis disappeared into her hot wet cavern.

Her vaginal walls pulsed around his flesh and he clamped his jaws shut to keep from groaning out loud at her wonderful tightness. Before he could start thrusting, she closed her legs, increasing the pressure and thus escalating the pleasure on his hard erection. Then she began to move her pelvis back and forth in slow motion.

Red hot lightning zipped along his shaft and slammed into his gut. This time he couldn't stop the moans escaping his mouth.

Leaning over, he palmed her soft breasts in his hands and began massaging her tight nipples and pulling on the rings. He smiled at her sharp exhalations as he pushed her breasts together, kneading them until she whimpered for mercy.

Blood pumped furiously through his veins as she kept up the slow sensual thrusts of her pelvis against him. Fighting the crazy need to spill his seed inside her cunt, he focused on pleasing Annie.

He increased the massaging on her mounds and grinned in satisfaction as they swelled in his hands. Her thighs tightened, sending another volley of raw lightning up his shaft.

He arched his hips against her and she bucked under his onslaught. He could hear her panting. Heavy and hard.

Savage pleasure ravaged his cock as he ground into her heat. Incredible pleasure spilled over his senses and his heart twisted with something he'd never experienced before. Something wild and wonderful. It urged him to ram his stiff cock deeper into her.

He fucked her with long drawn-out strokes until her cunt muscles began to contract around his stiff rod. Until she threw her head back and cried out for mercy. He ignored her and kept up the torturous strokes. He'd make sure she enjoyed this new sexual position. Make sure she enjoyed it a lot.

Fire burned his body as he watched himself withdraw. His cock throbbed in the fresh air. Lust encouraged him to spear himself back into her slick insides. Her soft satin hole tightened around him, sucking him into her snug warmth.

Setting up a torturous rhythm of his own, it didn't take long before her muscles convulsed around his hard shaft. Beneath his hands her swollen breasts heaved frantically as she sucked in gasps of air. Her body began to shudder as an orgasm drew near. But he didn't want her to come yet. He'd make her wait. Make her teeter at the edge for just a little bit longer.

He continued to buck against her body. Fucking her harder yet not hard enough to make her come. He continued his thrusts and at the same time one hand left her breast, dipping between her legs.

She groaned wildly and her legs trembled as his fingers slid against her clit ring. He pinched and massaged her luscious nether lips. They swelled beneath his onslaught. He could smell her sexy arousal permeate the air. It urged him on.

Slamming his engorged cock back inside her, he scraped a nail over her pulsing pleasure bud. She screamed. Moisture dripped from her hot cunt. He withdrew and shoved himself inside her again. Scraping his nail gently back and forth until she thrust her hips backward at him, a clear indication she was ready to come. And he was damn ready too.

Her throaty moan ripped through the silence as his fingers slammed roughly against her burning flesh. Massaging her vigorously, it didn't take long before she came apart. Humbled that he could bring such pleasure to her, he watched in amazement as her body shivered violently and her erotic screams rent the air around them.

Feeling his own completion nearing, Joe clenched his teeth and rammed harder into her heat. A moment later he joined her screams with hoarse cries of his own as the intense pleasure washed over him and he emptied his seed into her.

* * * * *

Annie watched as one by one the circling vultures disappeared from the bright afternoon sky. It meant only one thing. The hunt camp was now free and she could lead him there so he could pick up the trail that would eventually lead him back to his own kind.

Thinking about him being reunited with his own people should have made her happy. It didn't. As a matter of fact fear, raw and ugly, rolled inside her. Fear that he would leave her. Fear that she would never see him again.

At this very moment she was curled safely in Joe's powerful arms, lying on the soft warmth of the moss-covered rock. Safe from danger. But not safe from her fears.

She didn't want to wake him. Didn't want them to head for the camp. Most of all she didn't want him to leave her. He'd made no mention of where he would take her. No mention that he wanted anything more than sex from her. Not that there could be anything more. According to their laws, women could only take women as mates. Males were not mate material. Yet deep in her heart, there was an unexplained urge to make Joe her mate.

Perhaps the seeds had been sown when they'd held hands yesterday. Joe had explained males and women walked side by side. Lived together. Unbelievable. She would have to ask him more about the part of the world he came from. Up until now she hadn't had a chance. They'd been running from the women of the hub and from each other. Using all their free time to have sex. Perhaps it was a way to not face the truth of her situation. The truth being if he decided he didn't want her after all there would be no more strong arms curling around her body making her feel safe. Worst of all there would be no more lovemaking.

She'd been thinking about Joe throughout the night and throughout today. Up until now she'd managed to keep a handle on her emotions. After all, he was just a male. He shouldn't even be affecting her emotions. Unfortunately he was. He'd been the only male that had made her come apart. Mentally and physically. He was unbelievable in the way he aroused her. It was more than just great sex. There was something strong and deep in the way she felt about him. She couldn't explain it. All she could say was she'd never felt this way about a male before.

And there was something in his eyes too. Something in the way he looked at her. No other male slave had looked at her with such strong emotion. Yet again, she couldn't put a name to that emotion.

Annie sighed in frustration and snuggled against his warmth. A new urgency swept over her. She needed to find a way to make him want her. Or at the very least take her with him to wherever he came from. The thought of never seeing him again was unacceptable. Deep in her heart she knew something inside her would die if they parted.

Chapter Fifteen

Joe Hero grimaced as he stepped onto another sharp rock that littered the shoreline of the river.

A good long soak in a hot tub is what he needed. Something to soothe away all the pains that invaded his body. Or better yet another round of hot and heavy sex with Annie. At least having sex would keep his muscles loosened up and his mind off what he should do about her.

His heart quickened as he watched her naked ass sway seductively in front of him. Resisting the urge to cup those luscious smooth ass cheeks he forced himself to remember the strange way she'd looked at him after one of their lovemaking sessions earlier. Something in the way she'd smiled at him had tugged at his heartstrings. Had made him feel lost and confused. Her look was a direct contrast to the delicious torture her body had freely given him as he'd plunged inside her hot cavern.

The way they had kissed afterward. Hot, intense kisses that had led to some more lovemaking until they'd finally fallen asleep wrapped in each other's arms.

"It was the Yellow Hairs, just like I thought." Annie said as they climbed up the low embankment and walked into the vulture-laden meadow.

Joe's stomach heaved as he passed the skeletal remains of a human. The thought that this body could be one of his brothers almost brought him to his knees until he spotted the thatch of brown hair on the skeleton's skull.

He sighed in relief. Not the same color as either of his brother's hair. And definitely not their size. From this person's thin frame he had most likely been a teenager.

"The Yellow Hairs don't leave many scraps behind," Annie said from ahead of him. "But they'll be back for the bones in a couple of days when the vultures have picked them clean."

"Too lazy to do it themselves?" he joked. Although laughter was the furthest thing from his mind, he had the obscene feeling he just might go nuts thinking about what would have happened if a herdful of cannibal blondes had captured him. Suddenly he got the feeling what he'd gone through with the Sperm Bank was just a walk in the park compared to what happened to this poor fellow.

The sight of the skeleton only made the urge to get back to the spaceship that much more insistent. He needed to find his brothers. Needed to get the hell off this planet.

"Let's grab that secret stash of grub and find the trail, shall we?"

"It'll be getting dark soon. We should make camp here," Annie said.

"The last thing on my mind is to sleep with a corpse, Annie."

She twisted around and looked at him oddly. "Is this the first time you've seen a dead body?"

"I've seen plenty of dead bodies, just not ones torn apart by cannibal women. How about you look for the food and I'll see if I can pick up the trail? Which way to the sea?"

She nodded to the east.

"Okay, I'll look for the trail and scout around for a good place to camp, away from the corpse."

Annie nodded and headed toward the far side of the clearing.

Joe scanned the clearing for the trail. If he played his cards right, by this time tomorrow night he'd be reunited with his brothers and the last few days would be history.

He couldn't help but grin as he imagined their faces when they saw Annie. He'd have to do something about covering her body too. His brothers hadn't been with a woman since they'd started out on this voyage. They might be so damn horny, it would be downright painful if they saw a naked woman.

Oh man! A beautiful woman would be the last thing they'd expect him to bring home.

As he surveyed the surrounding bushes, he caught a glimpse of cloth.

It felt rough to the touch as he picked it up. It looked similar to the sack containing their meager food supply. And thankfully it was just big enough to wrap around his waist to cover his nudity.

Inhaling deeply, he smiled. With the cloth protecting his privates from prying eyes he felt like a civilized human being once again.

The next step on the agenda was to find the trail back to the spaceship.

* * * * *

Annie's stomach grumbled violently as she spied the camp's wooden trap door that would open to the food cellar.

At this point she was willing to eat just about anything. Well, certainly not human flesh.

She scrunched up her face in distaste as she stepped over a sun-dried human pelvic bone the Yellow Hairs had obviously used as a seat in front of a campfire.

Perhaps she'd find a hearty dish of dried berries and pig sprat in the cellar?

The bread and raisins she'd collected last night before they'd run were almost gone. If there wasn't any food in the cellar, she'd probably break down and cry or at the very least do some serious hunting for a vulture or two.

Vultures didn't taste that great. A bit stringy, but she'd eaten a few when food had become scarce.

Cool air slapped against her face as she lifted the food cellar door and descended into the gloomy interior. If the Yellow Hairs hadn't left any food here, she'd have to have a chat with their Queen.

Annie bit her bottom lip in frustration. She couldn't do that. She was now an outlaw. If she got caught…

Oh God, now she knew how Joe felt.

Trapped.

Frustrated.

Angry.

There was no way she was going to be put on a fucking machine and made to bear babies for the hub.

The thought of abandoning those women and babies in the prison weighed heavily on her mind. There was nothing she could do now. Her dream job was gone forever. She had been so close. Could taste the victory. But now it was over. She'd never be able to hold the tiny newborns in her arms. Never be able to watch the babes as they suckled from their mothers' breasts or teach the female children how to hunt or encourage them to follow their own dreams.

She wiped a stray tear from her eye and sniffed back a sob.

Freeing Joe had been the right thing to do. She couldn't let herself drown in her own selfishness. She'd done what felt right, even though everyone else believed she'd been wrong.

When it came down to it, *she* had to live with her own decisions, no one else. If she hadn't followed her own principles the rest of her life would have been miserable.

At least now she had a little happiness with Joe. How long it would last was anyone's guess. If he decided he didn't want to take her with him to wherever he came from, she'd survive. It would be a lonely existence but she could do it.

"A bag of food for your thoughts."

Annie froze as the familiar female voice sailed through the opening of the cellar. She whirled around to find the silhouette of Jacey, the Queen, blocking her exit.

Hysteria ripped along the edges of her mind. She clamped down on it. The thought of screaming a warning out to Joe was at the forefront, along with fighting hand to hand with the Queen. But the Queen was very experienced in hand to hand combat. Annie wasn't. If she screamed for help, Joe would come. And the Queen would capture him too.

"What are you doing, Annie? Why are you leaving me for a mere slave?" The Queen's voice was sharp, commanding.

Anger burst inside her and she started toward the Queen.

"Why can't you leave us alone?"

"Do you know what you've done, Annie? The council has put a price on your head. They want you dead."

The breath in Annie's lungs halted. Dead? No one had ever had a death price put on her head. At least not in her hub.

Despite her best efforts, Annie couldn't stop her legs from shaking with fear.

"So, you've come to take me back then. To watch them kill me."

Annie braced herself to fight as the Queen walked down the dirt steps toward her. She came to a stop a couple of feet away. The Queen smiled softly.

"No. I came to warn you." She reached out and Annie flinched as the Queen's warm finger gently fondled Annie's left nipple ring.

"To warn you and to give you another chance. I like you Annie. I want to help you."

"If you can help, help us both. Or there isn't anything I want to hear from you."

Jacey grimaced. "So, I'm too late then. I thought I might be. I watched how you allowed him to take you from behind by the river. You were taught better than that, Annie. You should never let the male have the dominant position."

The thought of the Queen watching Joe make love to her made Annie sick to her stomach. The urge to slap her was so urgent, Annie almost did it. Her upbringing stopped her. No one hit the Queen. Annie might be on the run but the Queen was still her boss. And the boss was allowed to do whatever she wanted to any female she picked.

She forced herself to hold perfectly still as the Queen's warm hand slid over the bottom curve of her breast. Only days ago the caress might have aroused Annie. It did nothing to her now. Nothing except make her angry.

"Joe said you saw us last night and that you let us go? Why?"

"I want to speak with the male."

"Never."

"He's a male, Annie. You tell him I want to speak with him and he'll do it."

"No, Jacey! He's a man! He has a mind of his own! You can't force him to do what he doesn't want to do."

A confused smile twisted the Queen's lips. It was a smile Annie didn't much like.

"Then you convince him, Annie. Convince him to talk to me. Perhaps I can convince him to return with us."

"No." She said the word so quickly it made the Queen blink in shock. Obviously she hadn't expected to be turned down.

Annie stuck her chin out in defiance. "No, I won't do it."

A pained expression ripped across the Queen's face. It made Annie sad. Made her wish she hadn't hurt Jacey's feelings. But she had and there wasn't anything she could do about that. She would protect Joe any way she knew how. Even if it meant offending her Queen.

"Fine," the Queen snapped. "The next time he's fucking you and you're both not looking over your shoulders and you get captured, don't come running to me for help."

The Queen turned and walked stealthily up the dirt steps.

Annie watched her disappear in the oncoming dusk. Her mind whirled crazily. Her heart pounded in her ears. The urge to run almost overtook her but she remained steadfast in the coolness of the cellar.

She needed to warn Joe. Needed to find him and get him out of here.

Quickly she ran her hands along the dark shelves in search for food. Her fingers brushed against something. Without seeing what was there she began stuffing the items into the grub bag.

A moment later she scrambled up the cellar's dirt steps and peeked out into the evening dimness. Nearby, the ugly vultures nibbled on the male skeleton. Tree branches moved in the hot evening breeze and birds chirped gaily here and there. Other than that, she detected no other movement. The Queen was gone.

And there was no sign of Joe.

Her thoughts tumbled together in a mass of fear. Had they captured him? Taken him away from her? She ached to call out to him. To see if he would answer. But she knew she had to remain silent. Cautiously she slipped out of the cellar and stepped into the gloomy twilight. Her back tingled as she imagined a bullet crashing through her spine.

Thankfully nothing happened.

She sprinted to the nearest tree line. Once there, Annie headed toward the area where she'd last seen Joe.

Chapter Sixteen

Joe had just found the east trail when he spotted Annie running toward him.

"We have to leave!" she gasped as she barreled into him. Her eyes were wide with panic.

"What's wrong?"

"The Queen. I saw her! She's found us."

"You saw her? Where?" Automatically his gaze searched the surrounding meadow. He saw nothing.

"In the cellar," Annie breathed.

"Did she see you?"

"I talked to her. We have to go. Now!" Her eyes were frantic as she grabbed his hand and began pulling him along the darkening trail.

"What did she say? How did you get away?"

"She let me go. Oh Joe, we've got to get you out of here."

Dammit!

"Any place around here where we can sleep without being seen? First light we can pick up the trail."

"The gully. I think we can make it there before darkness hits. But we have to hurry."

Joe grabbed the heavy sack from Annie. "Lead the way," he instructed.

It took Annie only minutes to have them secured in the gully behind the dark remnants of an old burnt out tree.

He watched Annie carefully. She sat cross-legged in front of him, the grub bag between her legs. Her full breasts bounced lightly in the increasing darkness as she searched the contents and handed him dried berries and another handful of dried meat.

Despite her rapid breathing and the occasional sounds of her swallowing her meal, she was quiet. Too quiet.

"What did the Queen say?" he finally asked, breaking the strained silence.

He heard her swallow. Could feel her fear zip through the warm night air.

For a long time she didn't speak and when she did he heard the tremble of terror in her voice. "She wants you."

He grinned. "Did you tell her I'm already taken?"

"This is serious, Green Eyes."

"C'mon, if she was serious she would have given us away last night and you said she just let you go. She's playing with us. If she was serious about taking me, her women would be scrounging around looking for us."

"I mean she *wants* you."

Joe swallowed the piece of dried meat that tasted oddly like beef jerky.

"She told you that?"

"No, but I'm a woman. I know these things."

"I see. Woman's intuition," he could barely keep himself from smiling. "Are you jealous?"

"Should I be?"

Oops, looks like her claws were coming out.

"What exactly did she say?"

"She wants to talk to you. Tonight."

Joe blinked in disbelief. "Why?"

She inhaled and moved against him. One of her soft breasts flattened against his arm. He could feel her rapid heartbeat pound violently against his flesh.

"She wants to fuck you."

"She said that to you?"

"No, but why else would she be following us without her entourage?"

"I thought you said she's only allowed to take a female mate?"

"She is. But what the others don't know...If she can have you without anyone knowing about it...You wouldn't fuck her, would you?"

"Of course not. What the hell kind of question is that?"

Her tense body seemed to relax a bit at his answer.

"She say anything else?"

"I told her you couldn't talk to her and she left."

"We just met and you're already bossing me around."

She smiled and cuddled closer. "You don't like me this way?"

"If I didn't like you this way, I wouldn't be here, Annie."

She seemed pleased with his answer.

He drew her into his arms and they lay down on the warm ground.

"I'm tired of running, Joe," she whispered. Exhaustion drenched her voice. "So tired. We need to sleep. We need to get moving at first light."

"Annie—"

A warm finger touched his lips silencing him.

"Shh. Don't talk. Just sleep."

Sleep?

Shit!

Now he knew something was wrong. Up until now all she'd wanted from him was sex.

"Don't tell me you're *that* tired?" he teased.

"I'm not *that* tired, Green Eyes. I'm never *that* tired. It's better we keep quiet. Don't draw attention to ourselves."

She had a point. They weren't the quietest lovers. If they started having sex anyone could hear them and their hiding place would be revealed. Besides, under the circumstances sex was the furthest thing from his mind.

The Queen was lurking around out there somewhere and she knew they were here too. He couldn't help but wonder why the Queen had let Annie go so easily or why she wanted to speak with him. Surely Annie was mistaken about the woman wanting him to have sex with her?

Or was it just some of Annie's insecurities coming out? It was totally understandable. She knew next to nothing about him. She thought he was from this planet. How in the world was he going to explain he was from Earth? Would she still want him if she found out he was pretty much an alien?

The question burned into his brain with razor sharpness and he shifted his body around in the darkness.

Curling an arm beneath Annie's soft shoulders, he cradled her tenderly and inhaled her sweet feminine scent. God, she smelled so damned good it was sinful.

Immediately she cuddled closer to him, burying her head into the crook of his neck. Her warmth was intoxicating and despite his best intentions he could feel himself going hard for her.

He swallowed and forced his voice to stay calm as he whispered into her hair. "Go to sleep, Annie. I'll take first watch."

She nodded and said nothing but he could feel the tremors of fear still coursing through her body. He ached to ask her to tell him again what exactly the Queen had said in case she had forgotten something.

He decided to keep silent. She needed sleep. They both needed sleep. They could discuss this tomorrow when they were far away from here and they didn't need to keep quiet.

It took a long time for the trembling in her body to subside. Finally her breathing grew shallow and steady and she fell asleep.

Darkness fell like a heavy blanket over the narrow gully and with it came the night sounds. A small creature slithered through the nearby weeds. Wings of some nocturnal bird fluttered overhead. There was no other sound. No other indication someone might be around except... Joe sniffed the air and the blood in his veins froze.

Wood smoke!

Shit!

Gently he moved Annie out of his arms. He sat up and waited to see if he could hear anyone talking.

Absolute silence. And yet the delicate scent of wood smoke hung in the air.

Making sure she was still asleep, Joe leaned over and kissed Annie gently on her forehead, then got up and crept up the nearby embankment.

The meadow was aglow with a white glaze, compliments of the full moon. Fireflies flickered but he saw no one or nothing that would produce the smell of wood smoke.

Following the scent, he kept to the darkness and silently trekked along the tree line until he came to the gurgling river.

Up ahead, on the rocky shoreline, a campfire glowed. Orange sparks shot into the air. In front of the campfire a lone woman sat on the log.

Not just any woman, but the Queen.

And she was naked as the day she was born.

"I'm glad to see you decided to come, slave," she called out.

Damn! How did she know he was here? He'd been exceptionally quiet as he'd come upon her.

"Come out. I am alone. You have my word," she said.

Joe remained silent as he surveyed the dark surroundings. Nothing moved. Nothing seemed out of the ordinary. No sounds except the gentle lapping of waves on the river's bank and the crackle of burning wood.

Stepping closer, Joe made sure he stayed clear of the circle of light the campfire cast.

"Come closer, slave." the Queen ordered.

"I'm fine right here."

Her eyes pierced the darkness and she frowned. "What are you wearing? Don't you know it is against the law for a slave to wear clothing?"

"I'm not a slave."

"All males are slaves."

"Not this one, honey."

Her frown vanished. She smiled sweetly and patted the log beside her. "Come, sit with me. We have things to discuss."

"What things?"

"Annie's freedom for one."

"She's already free," Joe said as he cautiously approached the Queen.

He was a sitting duck entering the campfire light like this but he needed to know why the Queen had followed them without her women.

"There's a price on Annie's head. A death price."

His guts tightened at her words and she craned her neck to look up at him. "I have a proposition for you. A way you can gain her freedom."

"What's that?" he asked cautiously.

"I want you to fuck me."

Joe's breath backed up into his lungs. Son of a bitch. Annie had been right!

He allowed his eyes to rake the Queen's breasts. They were full and luscious. Large nipples. The rest of her was like something out of a *Playboy* magazine. Curvy hips. Flat stomach. Cute belly button. Clean-shaven pussy. Long muscular legs.

She was a looker, but she didn't turn him on the way Annie did.

"And if I do? How does this make Annie free?"

"I'll go to the council. Tell them to give Annie a second chance. She can come back home. She can have the job I promised her."

"Where I come from, sleeping with the boss to get a job is illegal."

"Where do you come from, male?"

"It's better you don't know."

She ripped her intense gaze from his face and looked up into the star studded sky.

"From up there somewhere?"

He visibly jolted. How the hell did she know? As if she'd read his mind she smiled and said, "I'm the Queen. It's my business to know about planets and space explorers."

"Then you know there are other worlds out there."

"I know."

"How do you know?"

"The ancient books tell us. The Queens have access to all of them."

"Including access to guns and computers. Why don't you share your wealth of knowledge with the rest of your people? Why keep them in the dark?"

"Our ancestors decided long ago the general public would be better off with limited use of technology. They didn't want us to become like the male race."

Joe couldn't help but frown at the disgust in her voice. "What happened to them?"

"Same thing that happens to all inferior species. They slowly go extinct or kill each other off or are killed by their enemies. In case you hadn't noticed, the males are rare on our planet."

"Why?"

"We feel it is best to keep them at a minimum. Only a certain number are produced."

"Ah yes, your famous prison system."

"You disapprove?"

"Forcing women to have babies when they don't want them is obscene."

"It's punishment for wrongdoing. No different than your prison systems where people are incarcerated against their will for years and sit with idle fingers producing nothing."

Shit! How did she know about Earth's ancient prison system?

"Listen lady, this is not the time to chat about the social similarities of our planets. I want to know why you've been following us? Why do you want me in particular? Why not just get any male slave?"

"I watched you and Annie together yesterday when you took her under the waterfall. Watched you two in the ferns and then again today by the river. I saw what you did to her. The different positions. I saw the bliss on her face. I want you to give it to me too."

"I'm sorry Jacey, but it doesn't work that way. It goes deeper than just having sex."

She pouted. "I don't understand."

"Chemistry. A man and a woman have to have some sort of an attraction to one another. They need to like each other. They have to be willing to do things for each other. Willing to protect each other from harm. They work like a team."

"Annie, Cath, and I would have been a team if you hadn't come along. Why do you think I gave her the rings? She was mine." Anger sparked her words.

"She's not yours to keep or to give away, Jacey. She's a person with a mind of her own. You can't just expect her to come to you simply because you'll give her the dream job she wants. That's called buying a person's love. You're not earning it."

"Are you lecturing me?"

"No, just call it some friendly advice. Now, you mentioned something about a price on Annie's head?"

"The council has ordered Annie to be put to death after she is captured."

Joe's stomach sank. "You're the Queen. Don't you have a say in this? Can't you help her?"

"If you do what I want, I can change the council's decision. But you'll have to come back too. The women want you."

"Thanks, but no thanks. Not after the last welcome I got. I'm not eager to experience another round."

"You'll be well taken care of. You'll have many women every day. They will pleasure you. I'll even allow Annie to visit you secretly any time she wants."

"I can have her anytime I want now, why should I change that?"

The Queen frowned and stood up. She was a tall woman. Taller than him. For some strange reason he had the feeling she'd be a perfect match for his middle brother, Ben. Joe shook the thoughts away.

Before he could stop her she reached out and unsecured the knot holding the cloth he'd fashioned around his waist. It dropped away from him allowing her to see his nakedness.

Her eyes widened with appreciation as she gazed hungrily upon his privates.

Despite his urge to cover himself, he didn't. The last thing he wanted was to give her ammunition that some Earth males didn't like to be on display...unless it was in front of someone they cared about.

"I want you inside me," she breathed.

She made a move to touch his penis but he grabbed her wrist and pushed it away.

"You don't always get what you want, lady."

She smiled seductively. Suddenly he felt sorry for her. Sorry that she had to throw herself at him this way.

"I told you Jacey, I'm not interested. Now, if you came at me with a better offer to free Annie..."

Without warning she curled her arms around his neck and kissed him, cutting off his words. Her hot body melted against him and her moist mouth moved expertly over his lips. When her velvety tongue came crashing through his lips he clenched his teeth preventing access.

He grabbed her shoulders and broke the kiss.

"I have to admit, you're a good kisser," he whispered, "Probably good in the sack too. But like I said, I'm with Annie."

The Queen blinked in confusion.

"But I'm the Queen," she snapped.

"I don't care who you are. Annie and I are together. Nothing you do or say can tear us apart."

The shocked look on her face gave him little satisfaction. Slowly her arms slid from his neck. Before he could blink, she slapped him. Hard. He winced at the sharp pain searing through his left cheek.

He made no move to retaliate. He'd never hit a woman in his life and he wasn't about to start now.

"You turn down my offer! You insult me! What kind of a male are you?" she gasped.

"A free one."

Her eyes sizzled with anger. "The next time you're pulling on Annie's nipple rings and fucking her, be sure to keep an eye over your shoulder because you'll never be safe as long as you're free."

"I'll take that as the warning I'm sure it was meant to be. Now if you'll excuse me, I have to be going."

She said nothing as he reached down and yanked his breech clout from the stones where it had fallen. Without looking at her, he strolled casually up the rocky shoreline.

Inside, his guts were stretched tight. He got the feeling that any minute a group of screaming women would erupt from the nearby bushes and ambush him.

Nothing happened.

When the darkness of the nearby bushes crept in around him, Joe sighed with relief and sprinted for the gully.

And for Annie.

Chapter Seventeen

Early the next morning Annie and Joe hit the trail to the ocean. They moved quickly and quietly, neither speaking more than a few words at a time. Since yesterday's meeting with the Queen, Annie had remained quiet. The longer they were on the trail the quieter she got.

He wondered if perhaps she was thinking about what she'd left behind. Her dreams. Her way of life. Her almost mates.

His guts knotted at that last thought. She must have really wanted her dreams to agree to those rings and to agree to have sex with Cath and the Queen. He had nothing against lesbianism. To each woman her own, but Annie?

He never would have figured. But then again, it was her way of life, wasn't it? It was the way these women had been raised. To bow to their Queen's wishes. To take females as mates and use males as sex slaves.

Last night he'd gotten lucky with the Queen. Lucky that she didn't have a passel of women in the bushes ready to cart him off to sex slave hell.

Odd that she was out here all alone. Even odder that she'd tracked them this far. So why in hell hadn't she just sent her women after them and captured Annie and him? What was she up to? Besides trying to get him to make love to her.

As he traipsed along the trail he scanned his surroundings. Was the Queen following their trail right now? Was she planning on tracking them directly to the spaceship so she could catch his brothers too? If she was, she'd have a hard time of it. He'd been busily covering their tracks.

"Over there." Annie suddenly pointed to a dip between two large hills.

Joe lifted his head and followed Annie's gaze.

Golden sparks shone off dark blue waters beneath the late afternoon sun's rays.

"The sea?" he asked hopefully.

"Freedom Sea."

"How long before we reach it?"

"Before sunset."

Excitement ripped through Joe. By sundown he'd hopefully see his brothers. When he met up with them, he'd hug them like crazy. Dammit, he could hardly wait. Grabbing Annie's hand, he tugged her along the trail.

He was going home!

* * * * *

Standing on the sandy beach, Annie's mouth dropped open as she stared at the strange looking metal building in front of her. Silver in color, oval in size, it seemed about the same size of Cath's Slave Training cabin, if not bigger. Red, blue, and white markings with stars and stripes took up one quarter of it.

"What is it?" she whispered.

She held onto Joe's arm wondering why in the world he wasn't as afraid of it as she was. He seemed unmoved by the odd looking building. He just kept staring at it. His lips turned down into a frown. A frown she didn't much like.

"This is kind of my home away from home."

She grimaced. It looked sterile. Not at all cozy like her own hub house. But perhaps with a few flower boxes on the two windows...

"It looks...different."

"I don't think my brothers are here."

"All three of you live here together?"

The frown he'd been toting disintegrated into a smile.

"Annie, there's something I really need to tell you, but first let me show you the inside. C'mon." Tugging on her hand, he led her up the steps and to the door.

Here he stopped on a metal platform where a few lit numbers shone on a black console. The console looked oddly similar to the one inside the Queen's hub home where she kept all her duty scrolls and technology secrets that were reserved for Queen's eyes only.

Annie knew a higher technology existed. She was a doctor and had access to certain elaborate computers and medicines, so this computerized console didn't shock her.

Actually it excited her. It meant Joe came from a world of technology. She'd always been curious about the Queen's technology. At one point in her life she'd even considered applying for the position as a Queen, but her medical calling was higher.

She watched Joe place his palm on a small hand-sized computer screen and the door to the metallic building slid open.

"How'd that happen?"

"The computer has our handprints on file. It's the only way we can gain access."

"How impressive."

He smiled and tugged her inside.

Annie's eyes widened at the spectacular sight.

Colorful lights blinked here and there on white consoles. Three overstuffed green chairs sat in front of a large window that overlooked the ocean. In a far corner three cubicles with glass windows over them displayed comfortable looking beds.

Joe let go of her hand and sat down in one of the cozy looking chairs.

"Have a seat," he instructed as he proceeded to press some of the buttons on the console in front of him.

When a sexy female voice echoed through the room, Annie frowned and Joe smiled.

"Welcome back, Joe," the sultry female voice said.

"Hello Ashley."

Ashley? Who in the world was Ashley? His lover? Confusion and anger ripped through Annie. It was the same awful feeling she'd experienced last night when she'd discovered the Queen kissing Joe.

She'd awakened to the smell of wood smoke and much to her horror Joe wasn't lying beside her. Following the scent, she'd come to the river's edge and watched the Queen rip the piece of clothing from Joe's body. The Queen's hungry gaze as she'd peered upon Joe's nakedness had spawned a strange feeling inside her. A feeling she didn't like.

The awful sight of the Queen kissing Joe had made her run. Made her want to keep running until Joe could never find her. Instead, she'd headed back to the gully where she'd curled up and cried softly until she heard his soft footsteps. Pretending to be asleep, anger churned inside her when she smelled the Queen's scent all over him. She'd wanted to accuse him of betraying her. Of falling into another woman's arms so easily.

Why had he kissed her? What had the Queen said to him? And why hadn't Joe told her he'd visited the Queen?

Annie bit her bottom lip in frustration. Joe was a male, for heaven's sake. She shouldn't be feeling this way. She should have expected he would be sexually aroused by the Queen. She was a beautiful woman. He was a sexually active male. No matter how hard she tried though, she still felt as if he belonged only to her.

The sexy Ashley's voice broke into Annie's thoughts.

"You have three messages waiting for you, Joe Hero."

She watched Joe lean forward in the large recliner chair. Anxiety riddled his handsome face. "Bring 'em on, Ashley."

"Message One from Ben Hero. Dated four days ago." Her voice faded and instantly a man's deep voice echoed throughout the room.

"Joe! Where the hell are you? We got lost for a day but when we came back to the ship, you were gone. We followed your trail and found your gear stashed in some bushes near a river's edge but couldn't pick up your trail after that. We sure as hell hope you didn't drown, big buddy. We're going back out to track you tomorrow. If you show up here, stay put." The man's voice ended and Ashley's voice came back.

"Message Two from Buck Hero. Dated three days ago."

Another male's voice shot through the room. This one sounded worried. It wasn't the same voice as the previous message.

"Jeepers, Joe. I blew it big time. Ben's missing. We took off in different directions trying to find you. When Ben didn't come back I trekked out a day's walk north of here along the shoreline where he was searching for you. Stumbled upon women's footprints in the sand. Lots of women. But I lost Ben's footprints. I'm going back out again tomorrow to see if I can find him. If you get back here, stay here until I come back. Or hell, at least leave a message that you were here and tell me where you went." His voice clicked off into silence.

Annie's heart clenched as the frown on Joe's face deepened.

"Third message. Two days ago."

Buck Hero's amused voice erupted through the room.

"Hey Joe. Me again. I'm using my hand-held comm-link to relay this message. I've picked up Ben's trail again, heading northwest. Footprints indicate he's got company. Near as I can figure it's a group of five women. If you get this message stay put at the ship until I get back. If I don't come back…well it means I'm partying with a passel of beautiful women…don't wait up."

"End of messages, Joe."

"Thank you, Ashley." Joe leaned back in the chair. The frown he'd been carrying deepened until alarm zipped through Annie.

"I've got a bad feeling about all this, Annie. There have been no more messages from Buck. It could be he's simply out of range or maybe they got him too. Which tribe lives up the northeast way?"

"The Breeders."

"Forgive me for asking, who are the Breeders?"

"They raid hubs and take the males. They sell them to the highest bidders at the yearly auction."

"Are they dangerous?"

"They don't kill like the Yellow Hairs. If your brothers are captives of The Breeders, they won't be killed. Males are too valuable. The Breeders will train them to pleasure women. They are a relatively peaceful group. They use sex as a weapon."

"Meaning?"

"Withholding sex is punishment from what I've heard."

"Lovely. Ben won't like that. Could never keep his hands to himself for long. Buck on the other hand is like me."

To her surprise, he reached out and yanked her into his lap. "A one-woman man."

Arousal coursed through her as his large hands framed the side curves of her bare breasts. Annie fought the excitement erupting through her body. Before she got any deeper involved with Joe, she needed to get some answers.

"Joe. Don't."

A little frown made the corners of his lips dip downward. "What's been bothering you, Annie? Why have you been so quiet today?"

"I saw you last night. With the Queen."

Beneath her, Joe stiffened.

"Why did you go to her? Why did you kiss her?"

"She kissed me. I didn't kiss her back. If you'd stuck around, you would have seen her slap me."

"She slapped you?" Annie couldn't help but giggle at the image.

"I told her I only had eyes for you."

"She must have been very upset. No one says no to the Queen."

"I said no and so did you. She was ticked."

"After she slapped you, what happened?"

"I came back to you." He breathed against her ear. His hot fingers curled around each of her nipple rings. Sparkling sensations rippled through her breasts.

"Is everything okay now?" he asked.

Annie nodded.

"But I'm sure you're upset with me for taking you away from your way of life. From your dreams."

"I have new dreams."

His eyes flared with passion. She could almost feel the heat of them as they caressed her skin. "What kind of dreams?"

She bit her bottom lip, feeling a little bit embarrassed. She'd never shared her dreams with a man before.

"You can tell me. You can tell me anything. What are these new dreams of yours, Annie?"

"Just dreams." She shrugged her shoulders in a nonchalant manner, not wanting him to know just how important her new dreams really were.

"Tell me," he whispered. She noted the tinge of desperation in his voice.

Without warning his head dipped and he took a nipple into his hot mouth. Sparks of delight erupted inside her belly as he sucked her ring. His teeth gently nipped at her aching bud until she found herself moaning.

"Am I in your dreams, Annie? Am I your dream lover?" His head moved to her other breast and he kissed the under swell in a teasing manner. His sensitive touch made Annie's heart do a few little flips that left her weak in the knees.

"You're my dream lover," he whispered. "The only woman for me. I want to make love to you."

She giggled. "Now? Your brothers might be back any minute."

"Then they'll get an eyeful, won't they?" He kissed the valley between her breasts. "Don't worry, I've set the door so they can't come in without my permission. Until then, we can play house."

"And if they don't come back?"

"We'll go looking for them."

Beneath her thigh she felt his shaft harden. It was all the encouragement she needed. Lifting her legs, she untied the knot of the flimsy breach clout hiding him from her. The piece of cloth fell away and Annie's mouth watered at the intoxicating sight of his solid thick erection.

"You like?" he whispered huskily.

"I can't get enough of you."

"That's what I like to hear, Annie. 'Cause I sure as hell will never get enough of you. Sit on me. Make love to me like you did our first day in the clinic. You were so hot and horny. So cute."

"Were?" she pouted.

"Are. You are so hot and horny and you'll always be so cute."

A strangled little moan escaped her lips as his heat-seeking fingers danced to the entrance of her cunt, then slid inside.

"I can't get over how wet you are for me," he growled.

Fire laced her when his hard fingers filled her. A moment later a calloused thumb rubbed against her pulsing nub, making her gasp from the incredible sensations coursing through her lower body.

"Ride me, Annie," she heard him whisper.

Her body protested when his thick fingers popped out of her.

On trembling legs, she straddled him. Lowering herself slowly, she felt the broad head of his pulsing rod slip between her nether lips and slide up inside her aching cunt. She took immense pleasure from the torturous way his hard flesh invaded her, stretched her walls, and filled her.

He gazed up into her eyes and Annie swallowed at the layers of emotions swirling there.

Need. Want. Lust.

Something else. Something tender and caring and...could it be love?

"When my brothers come home, I'm taking you with us." His voice was thick with emotion. "On the voyage back you can tell me all your dreams so I can make them come true."

Annie couldn't help but to feel all warm and fuzzy inside from his words and his hard cock.

"I know you want to hold babies in your arms, so we'll have our own babies. Lots of them. We'll raise them together."

Her very own children! It was beyond her wildest imagination. Beyond her wildest dreams.

Her hands reached out and molded over the length of his warm chest muscles. Feeling the power of muscles beneath his skin, she slid her fingers sideways and skimmed over his ribs, downwards past his narrow hips. A moment later her hands slipped beneath his buttocks and she tried to pull him upwards deeper into her.

"In a hurry, are you?" His breathing was shallow, tortured.

In seductive movements she began to gyrate her hips. The clit ring scraped against her flesh. It did a fantastic job in arousing her but the groan of pleasure that grumbled somewhere deep within his chest pleased her more.

"Ride me, Annie. Ride me hard," he moaned.

She did as he asked and rode his shuddering body hard. His erotic groans increased spurring her on.

She loved the intimacy of their connected bodies. Loved the scent of their sex as it filled the air around them. Most of all she loved the slick, smooth feel of his penis deep inside her.

His eyes were slumberous, unfocused as he watched her.

He'd slipped into his own world of sexual bliss and within moments she slipped into the same world. Waves of explosions twisted her body. Explosions that send her spiraling into the world of love, erotic convulsions and blazing desire. A world she wished she could stay in forever.

The End

About the author:

Lauren Agony and Jan Springer welcomes mail from readers. You can write to them c/o Ellora's Cave Publishing at P.O. Box 787, Hudson, Ohio 44236-0787.

Why an electronic book?

We live in the Information Age—an exciting time in the history of human civilization in which technology rules supreme and continues to progress in leaps and bounds every minute of every hour of every day. For a multitude of reasons, more and more avid literary fans are opting to purchase e-books instead of paperbacks. The question to those not yet initiated to the world of electronic reading is simply: *why?*

1. *Price.* An electronic title at Ellora's Cave Publishing runs anywhere from 40-75% less than the cover price of the <u>exact same title</u> in paperback format. Why? Cold mathematics. It is less expensive to publish an e-book than it is to publish a paperback, so the savings are passed along to the consumer.

2. *Space.* Running out of room to house your paperback books? That is one worry you will never have with electronic novels. For a low one-time cost, you can purchase a handheld computer designed specifically for e-reading purposes. Many e-readers are larger than the average handheld, giving you plenty of screen room. Better yet, hundreds of titles can be stored within your new library—a single microchip. (Please note that Ellora's Cave does not endorse any specific brands. You can check our website at *www.ellorascave.com* for customer recommendations we make available to new consumers.)

3. *Mobility.* Because your new library now consists of only a microchip, your entire cache of books can be taken with you wherever you go.

4. *Personal preferences are accounted for.* Are the words you are currently reading too small? Too large? Too...**ANNOYING**? Paperback books cannot be modified according to personal preferences, but e-books can.

5. *Innovation.* The *way* you read a book is not the only advancement the Information Age has gifted the literary community with. There is also the factor of *what* you can read. Ellora's Cave Publishing will be introducing a new line of interactive titles that are available in e-book format only.

6. *Instant gratification.* Is it the middle of the night and all the bookstores are closed? Are you tired of waiting days—sometimes weeks—for online and offline bookstores to ship the novels you bought? Ellora's Cave Publishing sells instantaneous downloads 24 hours a day, 7 days a week, 365 days a year. Our e-book delivery system is 100% automated, meaning your order is filled as soon as you pay for it.

Those are a few of the top reasons why electronic novels are displacing paperbacks for many an avid reader. As always, Ellora's Cave Publishing welcomes your questions and comments. We invite you to email us at service@ellorascave.com or write to us directly at: P.O. Box 787, Hudson, Ohio 44236-0787.

Printed in the United States
25546LVS00006B/1-96

9 781843 605669